D1310629

BLOOD TANGO

ALSO BY ANNAMARIA ALFIERI

Invisible Country

City of Silver

BLOOD TANGO

To Catherine

ANNAMARIA ALFIERI

With all best wishes,

Annamaria Alfieri

MINOTAUR BOOKS
A THOMAS DUNNE BOOK
NEW YORK

A THOMAS DUNNE BOOK FOR MINOTAUR BOOKS.
AN IMPRINT OF ST. MARTIN'S PUBLISHING GROUP.

www.thomasdunnebooks.com
www.minotaurbooks.com

Design by Steven Seighman

Library of Congress Cataloging-in-Publication Data

Alfieri, Annamaria.
    Blood tango : a mystery / Annamaria Alfieri. — First Edition.
        pages cm
    ISBN 978-1-250-00455-0 (hardcover)
    ISBN 978-1-250-02048-2 (e-book)
    I. Title.
    PS3601.L3597B57 2013
    813'.6—dc23

                                                      2013011729

Minotaur books may be purchased for educational,
business, or promotional use. For information on bulk purchases,
please contact Macmillan Corporate and Premium Sales
Department at 1-800-221-7945 extension 5442 or write
specialmarkets@macmillan.com.

First Edition: June 2013

10 9 8 7 6 5 4 3 2 1

For Kerry Ann King, who makes my heart dance!

ACKNOWLEDGMENTS

Thank you with all my heart to:

David Jay Clark, who went to Buenos Aires and kept me company in my research, again. Henry Tedeschi, who shared his memories of BA at the very moment of this story. He and his parents and sister take a fateful walk again in this book. Lida Borello, who made friends with me on a New York City sidewalk and then took me on two fabulous tours of Buenos Aires, which greatly enhanced the sense of place of this story. Toni Plummer, my astute editor, whose incisive questions inspired me to dig deeper and made this book better. Adrienne Rosado, my agent, who carries my work and my career forward with care and sensitivity. And especially to Jay Barksdale and the staff of the New York Public

Library, Stephen A. Schwarzman Building, a gorgeous marble palace of free knowledge open to all. *Support your local library!*

That week of October 1945 is a week of many shadows and many lights. It would be better if we did not come too close . . . we should look at it from farther away. However, this does not impede me from saying, with absolute frankness . . . that the light came only from the people.

—EVA DUARTE DE PERÓN, *LA RAZÓN DE MI VIDA*, 1952

There have always been crooks, schemers, and dupes, the happy, the bitter, idealists, and frauds.

—ENRIQUE SANTOS DISCÉPOLO, LYRICS TO "CAMBALACHE"

Dancing in the dark,
Till the tune ends
We're dancing in the dark. . . .

—SONG LYRICS BY HOWARD DIETZ

BUENOS AIRES
1945

WEDNESDAY, OCTOBER 10

Trouble was closing in on Buenos Aires—like a huge jaguar charging toward the coast from the vast interior plain of the Pampas, with blood in its eyes and mayhem in its heart.

On that day of the 10th, thousands of people made their way to the center of the most elegant capital in all of South America. Their goal: a rally at the intersection of Alsina and Perú, where nineteenth-century buildings of scale and grace had earned the city its sobriquet—Paris of the South.

Among the throngs were six—three women and three men—whose futures hung in the balance. Two were obscure girls, oblivious to the scent of the approaching beast. Two young men, with axes to grind, felt the giant cat coming and feared it. Evita Duarte prayed it would be an angel bearing gifts; she opened her heart as it neared. Juan Perón imagined he himself might embody its power and decide the fate of the nation.

On that cloudy afternoon in spring, Argentina's destiny was ripe for the picking. No one was happy with the government, not even the men who were running it. The country's divided citizenry had never chosen sides in the worldwide conflict just ended in Europe and Japan. The upper classes, who spoke Spanish but otherwise comported themselves like British aristocracy, had favored the Allies. The Axis-leaning generals of the military regime had no idea how to maintain their power after having backed the wrong horse in World War II. Every move made by either side—the army or the clamoring populace—merely increased the level of national dissatisfaction and confusion.

Turmoil had stalked the nation for over two years. Now chaos prowled ever nearer and threatened to grab Buenos Aires by the throat. It would take a week before the crisis played out and Argentina's destiny was sealed.

The event, which drew fifteen thousand, began as a seemingly innocuous occasion: a farewell rally to see off Juan Domingo Perón. Until the day before, Perón had been the most powerful, and therefore the most hated, man in Argentina: its vice president, minister of war, and secretary of labor. The populace massing in the plazas and storming along the *avenidas* had demanded his fall from grace. Finally, a reluctant President-General Edelmiro Fárrell deposed Perón. Many in the army hierarchy imagined that this sop to the protestors would actually save the day.

Colonel Perón, less put out than one would have imagined, approached the rally in the backseat of a chauffeur-driven, gleaming black Packard touring car; the speech he was about to give lay in his lap. He gazed out at the blooming jacarandas along the streets, the Beaux Arts apartment buildings, the leafy parks as they passed. He felt the jaguar nearing. Soon he would either become one with it, or it would bloody his dreams and devour his future.

The tiny, pensive woman next to him on the plush leather seat, his mistress, the radio soap opera actress Evita Duarte, held his hand and stared out the opposite window but took no notice of the elegant architecture and fancy restaurants. She clenched her teeth on her bottom lip.

Perón was angry with her. At home that morning, she had stamped and stormed over her colonel's loss of might. She wanted to keep quiet now, but her outrage threatened to boil over, again.

When General Avalos had come to their apartment, as President Fárrell's emissary, to demand Perón's resignation, she had tongue-lashed the miserable bastard. Insulting words had flown out of her mouth. Avalos had stared, stupefied, as if he had been scolded by a lapdog. Perón had not berated her for that outburst, merely raised his eyebrows. But she was sure he had been extremely displeased. She had gone too far.

She let go of Perón's hand and tugged the hem of her tweed skirt toward her knees. "Avalos calls himself the commander of a garrison? He's a stuffed cuckoo. He looked like a gnome standing next to you. If that parley in our living room had been a scene in a movie, everyone watching would have seen you as the tall, handsome hero and him as a squat dope, without brains or cojones. I don't know how you keep your temper with them, Juan. Why are you so calm?" She bit her lip again.

Perón took her little hand back into his and squeezed it hard. It did not seem to either of them purely an act of affection. He considered her. With her enormous power to sway ordinary people, she might help him regain his position, but her passion would be useful only if she contained and he directed it. Otherwise, her impulsiveness would destroy his balance as he walked a tightrope back to the seat of government. Everything depended on the purity of her belief in him. He had to be careful which of her strings he pulled. Best to keep her off balance for now: insecure enough to remain on the sidelines but sure enough of him to stay close and be ready to help when he wanted her. What a dance he had to perform to keep her within bounds. But if it worked, she would be worth it.

He reached into the left breast pocket of his suit jacket and took out a package of Gauloises and the gold cigarette holder his men at the War Ministry had given him for his fiftieth birthday. That was only two days ago—when he had still controlled the most important parts of the regime, including the president himself. Not anymore. Perhaps never again. He held the trinket out in the palm of his hand. "This may be the last such gift I receive," he said.

"You are tired," she said.

"I am discouraged." He gave her a regretful smile. "You are young. When you are young and tired, you feel tired. When you are old and tired, you feel old."

"You are not old," she said, though his age was just under double hers. "Perhaps you should take some time to rest."

"I think I need a permanent rest." The words were out of his mouth before he considered whether they would move her toward being more useful or less.

She took in her breath in alarm and looked at him in shock. Her heart skipped a beat.

"No, no." He waved his hand as if to erase what he had spoken. "I don't mean giving up on life. But we could go away, live quietly together, and not have to contend with all this turmoil. To Uruguay. To Paris, even, now that the war is over. We could have a nice time, just the two of us." He knew the image was a fantasy, a pretty picture he would never truly inhabit. It could, however, be a prize he dangled, a carrot to get her to control her temper. He watched her eyes in the rearview mirror in the center of the windshield. He could not tell if she was taking the bait. He put the cigarettes and holder back in his pocket without lighting up.

Evita heard longing in his voice. He spoke of a life for them together. She wanted that. She needed him. More than he needed her. Where would she go if she lost him? And where would her future go if he lost out? She wanted the safety a man of power could give. She deserved it after all she had suffered. "Will you abandon the poor workers?"

He patted the yellow foolscap pages of the speech on his lap. "I have one more gift to give them today. After this, I may be beyond helping them."

She almost called him a coward. She wanted to see him fight like a tiger. For his position. For what he could do for the poor. "What will those boys down in the slaughterhouses do without you to be their champion?"

He smiled. Her power would come from this anger at injustice. For now, he must kindle the flame without letting loose its fury—keep her off balance and tip her in the right direction when the time came. Like firing an artillery shot when the enemy was close enough to die. "If I have the poor workers' complete support, perhaps I will have the future we all want. Sometimes I think no one can destroy me if they are on my side."

She searched his eyes in the reflection for a clue to what he wanted her to say. She felt danger in the touch of their hands. If she pushed him too far, he would throw her over. She was not his wife. One word from him and she would be gone.

They never talked of marriage; they both knew why: as long as he needed the support of his so-called superiors, he could never marry such a wife: a common actress, especially an illegitimate child like herself. But she spoke about her origins to no one—especially not to him. For over a year now, he had defied the army's stuck-up morality and lived openly with her. She knew his fellow officers despised him for it. "Those army snobs have forced you out because of me. It's true, isn't it?" She bit her lip, as usual *after* she had said entirely the wrong thing.

He patted her knee. It was like her to think she was the

reason for everything that happened, but in this case she was more than half right. True, everyone in the country seemed to have one reason or another to get rid of him. The upper classes because he pushed through laws forcing them to pay their workers more. The crowds in the streets blamed the army for imposing the state of siege and suspending the constitution. They singled him out as the most visible symbol of military rule. The worst fools insisted he was a Nazi. How could he be a Nazi? He did not have a single drop of German blood in his body. Those who called him one were a bunch of communists. He sighed. All that was true, but his enemies focused more on her than on anything else about him. Which could be good as well as bad.

She shifted in her seat as the car turned south toward the center. His silence made her nervous. "Those disgusting vultures who oppose you," she said. "They deserve to be horsewhipped. Even a horse deserves better treatment than they do." She fingered the oversize ring on her right hand. She wanted the chance to seduce crowds for him, make them gather in the plazas and chant his name. She had talked on the radio about his greatness, but no woman could take a platform in public, especially a woman who was his mistress, not his wife.

He kissed the back of her hand. She was puzzled, off balance. Which was where he wanted her. For now.

———

While Perón's Packard left the sycamore-lined streets of the Barrio Norte and entered the commercial district, Lieutenant Ramón Ybarra, handsome and elegant in civilian clothes, carried his hatred to the rally by underground train. As he exited the Subte's A Line at the Perú Street stop, he looked up approvingly at the gray skies, so fitting for the mood of the nation. He wished he could draw a downpour from those clouds to wash out Perón's speech or, better yet, a lightning bolt to strike down both him and his actress mistress.

Ybarra had come to watch, firsthand, the next act in the drama that threatened to plunge the country into chaos. Earlier he had left the Palacio Paz, the army's headquarters in Buenos Aires and supposedly the center of its power, but these days the mahogany-paneled rooms seemed to Ybarra more like a dovecote for an emasculated flock of cowering pigeons. Over the past two years, his army superiors had allowed Colonel Juan Perón to dilute the army's power and to aggrandize his own. Whoever heard of a military government that supported Bolshevik labor unions? What the fuck had happened to the army's campaign for public morality? Could the military demand that ordinary people stop acting like animals if the most powerful man in the service lived openly with a common actress?

The downward spiral of the nation had been troubling Ybarra for months. But while the country tottered on the edge of an abyss, the senior officers had stroked their mustaches, talked about trouble brewing but had done nothing to quell it. Now they had forced out Perón, but was he gone forever? On would he return with more might than before?

The scene around Ybarra increased his fears. The streets were packed. There were thousands here. Perón, the clever bastard, had put his farewell gathering at a spot easily reached by many. If the rabble decided to bring their outrage to the seat of government, they would have only a few blocks to march to the Casa Rosada: a pink palace. Not a proper color for a national headquarters, but it seemed to suit the current resident. President Edelmiro Fárrell was more interested in women and song than showing force and ruling Argentina.

Ybarra pulled down the brim of his hat to hide his identity. Making sure he would not be recognized was one of his main objectives this afternoon. The other was to get the goods on Eva Duarte, evidence that she would fight to restore Perón to power. After those shameless paeans to her lover that she broadcast over the radio, Ybarra was sure the *puta* would stop at nothing to make sure her sugar daddy had the connections to keep her in the sweet life.

The tall lieutenant in the civilian suit moved with the throng down Perú to where a platform had been erected, complete with microphones and decorated with blue and white bunting and Argentine flags. As if Perón were a patriot. It made Ybarra want to vomit.

Suddenly, he could have sworn he saw Perón's mistress ahead of him in the crowd. Just there, a little blond in a straw hat. He was amazed. He had expected Evita to come, but he had imagined the little slut would arrive in Perón's fancy car. What could she be doing out here with the mob, wearing a green dress, and chatting with another girl, acting like the common woman she was? He tried to get a closer look but failed to make any headway in the press of people jamming the intersection.

Keeping his eye on the spot where he had seen her, Ybarra settled for a place on the fringe of the crowd, among a bunch of unionists carrying signs that said WORKERS' RIGHTS ARE HUMAN RIGHTS.

Why the bastard was being allowed to stage this farce was beyond understanding. The generals should have muzzled him, not given him a platform at government expense. And from the looks of the big square microphones and the heavy wires coming from them, Perón and his minions were going to broadcast whatever he said, so there would be no censoring him. This was a huge mistake.

Perón's Packard pulled up across the intersection, and the colonel got out. He was tall enough to be seen over the heads of his cheering supporters. When an old man in an ill-fitting suit appeared on the platform and started to fiddle with the sound equipment, the mob began to chant, *"Sindicato. Sindicato."* Others, not satisfied with praising their Trotskyite unions, took up the eminently chantable name of the son of a bitch who had raised their wages and used the business owners' money to buy their love. "Perón. Perón."

Ybarra craned his neck to see if he could catch sight again of the actress, but the crowd was too thick. As Perón mounted the stage, they surged forward, stamped their feet, and clapped their hands. "Perón, Perón."

The man of the moment approached the microphones to tumultuous applause. The *puta* was not with him. That must have been her Ybarra had seen in the crowd. Someone had had the good sense to keep her in her place—in a manner of speaking. If she was really kept in her proper place, she would have been cleaning someone's house. Or lying dead in a coffin.

The whole scene boiled Ybarra's blood.

On the other side of the chanting crowd, an equally angry Tulio Puglisi was one of the unionists in the ranks, shouting, "*Sindicato! Sindicato!*" only to be drowned out by people he thought misguided at best. They called not for justice for workers but for one man only. "Perón. Perón."

Too short to see over the masses, Tulio stood on the tips of his shoes—the best the leather workers of his union could produce—and fumed in his heart over this outpouring for a man he considered a devil.

At a ten-hour-long meeting of the various unions the day before, he had repeatedly begged the other officials to stand down from this circus, to wait until October 18, when they could organize a demonstration for something other than the power of Perón, Argentina's prime fascist. Puglisi had dragged out every possible argument: reminded them that their Juancito Perón fell in love with Mussolini before the war started; that, like his fellow army officers, he loved the Germans.

Tulio's friends had looked at him in horror. Many of them were cowed by the threat—present though not certain— that a person who spoke such thoughts could disappear and not be seen again. But Tulio's family had resisted intimidation in Italy, and right here in Argentina during the war, they had stood up to the fascists who with their Nazi counterparts had prowled immigrant neighborhoods, trying to force Germans and Italians to support their dictator-heroes. He was his father's son and no coward. What was it to be a leader if you refused to take a risk for what you believed?

The pro-Perón so-called unionists at that meeting had given him smug looks, as if they had his number. They countered his arguments with a laundry list of Perón's "gifts" to the workers: better wages and working conditions, paid vacations, free health insurance. True, the colonel had arranged those benefits, but with only one purpose—to enthrall the most ignorant among the union members.

"This is our moment to stop the fascist," Puglisi had declared, "while Perón is weakened. If we don't seal his fate now, he will make sure we never get another chance." The men around the table had looked away from him.

Finally, in desperation, he told them a secret he was not supposed to divulge. "My sister-in-law works for Bishop Coggiano. Perón is bringing in Nazis. She has seen them in the bishop's palace. They are moving here in droves. It's all controlled from the Vatican. German and Croat war criminals, using gold from the teeth of people they murdered to buy into our country. The bishop says we need them because they are anti-communist. Before we know it, the Fourth Reich will be ruling Argentina."

A hush fell on the proceedings after that, but he could not change their minds. The more he begged, the less they listened.

After the meeting, Tulio's cronies tried to gloss over the fact that he had said things that could get a man thrown in prison or worse. They slapped him on the back. "Oh, come on, Tulio," they said. "Tomorrow is his farewell rally. You should be glad to say good-bye to him if you believe he is such a dangerous character." Then they all disappeared, and he realized that even his closest allies were too afraid of what he had said even to drink a coffee with him.

Defiant in the face of intimidation, Puglisi had put on his best suit and shoes and come to this Perónist circus.

The platform his nemesis now mounted was festooned with blue and white bunting and Argentine flags flapping in the breeze on each corner, the colors of a country Tulio saw as doomed. Then he saw in the crowd Perón's lady friend. She had been praising him on the airwaves as if he were some sort of deity. Puglisi believed she could become a key player in this real-life drama, but he knew what his fellow unionists would say if he brought up that subject—that no one would take a soap opera actress seriously.

But Tulio Puglisi knew in his bones that stopping Eva Duarte could very well be the key to saving Argentina from fascism. He felt as if he were the only person in the country who knew that.

Near that platform in the center of the intersection, Jorge Webber, Perón's chauffeur, shadowed Evita. She was nervous today. She had spoken sharply to Perón in the backseat while Webber drove them. The colonel had left them in the car, saying Evita should stay inside the vehicle and telling Webber to keep her there with him. But as soon as Perón walked away, Evita got out of the car and ordered Webber not to accompany her. She spoke in that demanding way of hers. He held his tongue and followed her without her realizing it. He wondered how she could bear the stares of the people around her. Cranky as she was with him, he felt compelled to protect her. A few feet away from him now, she tapped her foot and looked at her red fingernails. He could tell she was trying not to bite her cuticles.

Over and over, people nearby recognized her and insisted on trying to talk to her. Their voices were mercifully drowned out by the sloganeering. Webber feared there were people here who hated her. He had heard what they called her behind her back. Sometimes he wondered that she seemed not to notice. It was his job to make sure they did not insult her.

Across the jammed street, near the cheering employees of the Secretariat of Labor, Luz Garmendia was delighted to have people try to talk to her. She smiled coyly at them and basked in their admiring glances, because they mistook her for the actress Eva Duarte. That she could pass for Evita had changed her life. Pride shone in the girl's dark eyes. Today, more than any other of her life, she felt whole and happy. She had always tried to act cheerful, but until she met Evita she had been sad for as long as she could remember.

After her mother died, when she was four years old, she had lived alone with her father and his mother. If she had been strong like Evita, she would have told her grandmother how bad it was to constantly remind a child what a burden she was to her father. And if Luz really were Evita now, she would have her father arrested for the beatings he had given his little girl anytime she showed any spirit.

At fifteen, she had run away to live with Lázaro, a man she met in the market who smiled and promised to marry her. For the first month, he had petted her and told her she was beautiful. Then, he, too, began coming home drunk and smacking her around. One night he choked her while she slept; she woke up unable to scream. Not even her father had done anything that bad, but she had had nowhere else to go. If she really were Evita, she would have him arrested, too, for breaking his promise.

Luz's life had been miserable until Señora Claudia, a dressmaker who lived in the apartment building where Lázaro worked as a gardener, had rescued her. That wonderful lady had found little Luz a room in a good woman's house and had given her a job in her elegant shop on Florida Street.

Luz had begun by cleaning, but before long she was taking out basting stitches and ironing dresses. The workshop was a paradise of colors and textures: blue, white, and silver brocade, soft fuchsia cashmere, thick tan English tweed, gossamer turquoise silk.

One day, Luz was unable to resist a black sheath gown she was pressing. It had a square neckline and slender skirt with a cunning slit at the front of the hemline that curved apart to reveal the lady's shoes. The dress was lined with cream-colored satin. Alone in the shop, Luz had taken the garment into the dressing room and slipped it on. It felt like water on her skin. She put on the high heels that were kept for customers to use when trying on long dresses. The shoes were several sizes too big for Luz's tiny feet. She shuffled out to the carpeted pedestal to see herself in the triple mirror. The gown looked as if it had been made for her. She had stared at her reflection and wondered what a girl would have to do for a man to catch one rich enough to buy her a dress like that.

At that moment Claudia Robles had opened the door and stepped into the fitting area. Luz let out a yelp, but she was frozen. She could not get off the pedestal and run away in the narrow skirt and flopping shoes. She burst into tears.

"No don't," Claudia called out. "Don't let your tears drop onto the silk." She grabbed a cloth from the bin where they threw the scraps and ran over to dry Luz's eyes. Then she stepped back and appraised the girl in the splendid gown. "It fits perfectly," she said. "You don't have her face or hair, but your bodies are identical. Look how that gown fits you. Even the length is just right."

"Who is it for?" Luz had asked.

"Evita."

Like a word in a magic spell, the speaking of that name began Luz's real life. For nearly five months now, rather than on a manikin, Señora Claudia had fitted all the actress's clothing on Luz's body. And she asked Luz to model for Evita and her sister and their friends when they came into the shop to pick up suits, day dresses, ball gowns, all the beautiful things an important woman needed. Evita said that rather than trying on the outfits herself, she preferred to watch Luz move in them. It gave her a better idea of the impression she made.

Evita was so kind. She taught Luz to walk and to sit like a lady in a play. And she gave Luz a large tip on each visit. Just a few days ago, she had given Luz the beautiful dress she had on at the rally today, an afternoon dress of spring-green lawn, with a narrow waist and a dirndl skirt that came just to the bottom of her knee, so that it showed the curve of her calf, but still looked demure. The buttons in a double row down the front were mother-of-pearl, the size of a one-peso coin. The short sleeves turned up in a cuff. Luz loved the way she looked in that dress here today with her now-blond hair, fixed in a style she had seen on the actress. Even her makeup—penciled eyebrows and bright red lipstick—matched what Evita always wore. Luz felt wonderful.

Earlier that morning, when she had met her friend Pilar, who worked with her in the dressmaker's shop, Pilar had said, "You look like the daughter of one of those dandies who arrives on the Calle Florida in a chauffeur-driven car to shop at Harrods for riding boots." But Luz knew better. She looked like Evita. And the glances of people around her confirmed that. She glowed with the conviction that many of those who stared at her thought she really was the lover of the man whose name they chanted, the beloved leader they were about to lose.

Pilar Borelli, Luz's co-worker, scanned the people around them for a different reason. Her wary eyes sought signs of danger. As they left the Subte and made their way to the intersection of Alsina and Perú, Pilar had caught sight of Miguel Garmendia, Luz's father, a man Pilar knew to be a threat to his sweet, star-struck daughter. Just the week before, Garmendia had come to the Club Gardel, where Pilar went to dance the tango. That night he had threatened to kill Luz.

By midnight on that Saturday, the Club Gardel had just gotten into full swing. The bar was packed with single guys eyeing the girls along the wall opposite. Though the dance floor took up most of the club's space, it was inadequate for the number of couples. The denizens of the troubled city seemed to have turned to their music and their dance as the only possible comfort in the face of imminent chaos. The longing in the melodies, the nostalgic, sometimes bitter lyrics matched the mood of the moment in Buenos Aires.

As the strains of "Caminito" ended, the seamstress Pilar

Borelli let go of the hand of Mariano, the singer everyone thought was her boyfriend. Often Mariano thought so himself, and sometimes she let him. Whenever he was not at the microphone he danced with her, and she seldom danced with anyone else though she hated the smell of the carnation he always wore in his buttonhole. He said it was his homage to the great tango singer, Carlos Gardel, but it reminded Pilar of her mother's funeral.

Mariano climbed onto the bandstand, whispered into the ear of Luis, the bandoneón player, and adjusted the big round microphone. Pilar turned toward the bar and immediately caught the eye of a heavyset man of about fifty making his way toward her with a look that seemed to say he wanted to dance with her. He was unsteady on his feet, had had too much to drink. She turned away, toward the sanctuary of the ladies' room, but before she could fight her way there, his heavy hand on her shoulder arrested her progress. The next thing she knew, he was slobbering a bunch of slurred words at her.

"I am sorry, I don't want to dance this one," she said and tried to continue on her way.

The man moved in front of her and gave a menacing look. "I am looking for my daughter," he said with a breath of gin.

Pilar, who had never met her own father, went chill. Surely this goon could not be him. "Do you know me?" she asked with trepidation.

"No," he growled, "but the bartender sent me to you." He poked his thumb over his shoulder.

Mariano's velvet voice sang out, *"La Canción de Buenos Aires."*

"Who are you, señor?" Pilar's voice shook. Her mother had told her her father's name before she died.

"Miguel Garmendia," he said.

Pilar's heart did not know whether to lift or sink. This brute was not her father, but he was the father who had brutalized her friend Luz.

He pointed his thumb at the bar again. "He told me you know my Luz. I want to know where she is."

"I don't know, señor," Pilar said.

He jutted his chin. "The bartender told me she has been in here with you. More than once." His eyes burned into hers.

Pilar looked down at the black-and-white checkerboard tile beneath her feet. Behind Luz's father, on the little stage, Mariano went on with his song. "I know her, but only slightly," she lied. She made her voice sweet. "I will tell her you are trying to reach her the next time I see her, if that will help. Does she know where to find you?"

Garmendia grabbed Pilar's elbow and squeezed it, sending a pulse of pain to her shoulder. "You tell her to come home, or else. Tell her I will kill her if she doesn't, and I will kill anyone who keeps her away." He let go of Pilar's arm and lurched to the door. She did not take her eyes off him until he disappeared up the steps and out into the street.

She went to the bar and berated Lorenzo, the bartender, for pointing Garmendia toward her. "Don't you ever let that animal in this club again," she said, as if she had the right to command him.

She could not bring herself to dance any more that night. She stayed at the bar, with her elbows on the white marble and her hands holding up her head. She drank more than was her habit and listened to the longing in the songs written by displaced people like her mother, who had forever left behind her loved ones in Italy to look for a life without the threat of starvation. In the new world, she had found food for her body, but also awful loneliness. In the end she had died young and left only a barely grown-up daughter behind.

Now, amid the cheering mob at the rally, Pilar's skin prickled with fear. Garmendia was here. If he found Luz, both girls would be in danger. Pilar could only hope the density of the crowd would protect them.

Suddenly the animated press of people around the girls went wild as Juan Perón, behind the microphones, raised his hands over his head and smiled warmly, nodding his approval at the adulation of the thousands surrounding him.

With a great flourish, he removed his jacket and slowly rolled up his sleeves. The crowd stamped, clapped rhythmically, and chanted the name of their jacketless hero. "Perón. Perón."

Many of the men near Ramón Ybarra took off their jackets, too, and twirled them over their heads, shouting, "Viva Perón!" Anxious that he not be spotted as an interloper, Ybarra pasted on an approving smile and attempted to subdue his outrage. Wherever men went in Buenos Aires, they were required to show respect by wearing jackets and ties. No restaurant or movie house in this elegant city would admit a man dressed in the disgraceful way Perón chose to appear before this crowd of lowlifes. Ybarra swallowed the spittle he would have preferred to spray on the cheering monkeys around him.

On the platform, the idol of the scum loosened his tie and held his hands aloft. The noise of the crowd swelled again and then finally subsided to near silence as he began to speak. The voice that came over the loudspeakers was deep and warm and entirely confident, the smile he beamed at them sunny and sincere. There was nothing about the man that would indicate that he had just been stripped of power. Surrounded by flying flags and the adulation of thousands, he spoke of liberty and the glory of their nation, of the power of the workers. His amplified voice echoed off the surrounding buildings, whose stately facades and refined appointments lent an air of importance to his fine words.

Ybarra winced when Perón's final gift to his sycophants elicited the wildest applause of the afternoon. Perón announced, in that irresistible voice, increases in wages for workers and an index tied to the cost of living, so that, according to Perón, the laborers who were ultimately responsible for the prosperity of the nation would not lose the gains they had made in the last three years. The bastard was reminding this mob, and anyone listening on the radio, of exactly what they owed to him, and only to him. "Perón. Perón."

———

General Fárrell, the president of Argentina, listened to the radio broadcast in the Casa Rosada three blocks away, as did General Avalos, commander of the garrison, in his office north of the city at Campo de Mayo, and the heads of oligarchic families in their marble halls of power and luxury. All realized that Perón had scored an enormously powerful parting shot. What he had just said had been heard by millions all across Argentina and could not be rescinded without unleashing mass revolt.

On the edge of the crowd, near the car, Evita Duarte placed her hands over her heart when she heard her colonel's words. He had not told her beforehand what he was going to say. Her whole being burned with pride and admiration. This man on the stage, her man, was the savior of the poor. And he was rubbing the noses of the bourgeoisie in their own shit and frustrating their attempts to destroy him. He was the most important, most valuable man in the country, perhaps in all of South America, and instead of being feted for the great leader he was, he was being tortured by a nest of snakes who had not an ounce of vision or leadership. Behind her admiration prickled a fear: this bold act of Perón's could be political suicide. She wanted to save him. She had more balls than any of his enemies. Someday she would make them feel her wrath. Whatever their treachery and lies did to him, she would never leave his side.

Perón made a brave show of enjoying the festivities, flashing his sunshine smile, but Evita saw anxiety in his body, like a caged animal's. He was an athlete, and when a fight was upon him, it showed in his gait: he moved swiftly with focus and intention, like the fencing champion he was, intending the épée for his opponent's heart. Now he clasped the hands of his supporters, but as a conciliatory man. There was no edge of threat in his demeanor. She knew he trusted the army's officers to follow their code of gentlemanly conduct and leave him to make a new future for himself. But she trusted none of them. Powerful people made up their rules as they went along, whatever worked for them, the way her brother used to declare different rules for boys and girls when he played games with her and her sisters. People who had the nerve to make up their own rules were the ones who won.

Evita punched her fist into her left hand. Perón's enemies should all be erased from history. Evita swore in her heart that they would be, if it took her last breath.

Tulio Puglisi, from his position at the back of his union's contingent, could not see the man behind the microphone, but he heard the impassioned speech and read between its vague lines an appeal to the workers to rise up for Perón, as if the whole idea of a union was for the workers to put their faith in one powerful manipulator, instead of in the collective. This rally was a miniature of the outpourings for Hitler and Mussolini that he had seen in the newsreels. If Perón's supporters swelled in numbers, Argentina would see adoring crowds exactly like those in Rome who had chanted, *"Duce. Duce."* But here they would clamor for "Perón. Perón."

Nauseated by the thought, Tulio turned away from the man with the winning smile, and he saw her again a little distance away, Eva Duarte amid the crowd, wearing a green dress and grinning with pride. It would have been more like her to stick close to her colonel, but perhaps she meant to place herself in the middle of the throng so that she could take its pulse. Evidently she expected to position herself as an ordinary person so that she might learn the best way to influence the workers.

But Eva Duarte was not a woman of the people. She may have started out working-class or less, but now she wore clothes from Florida Street and rode around in a chauffeur-driven Packard.

While Perón left the platform and plowed through the crowd toward his car, Puglisi tried to follow the actress to see what she would do next. The army may have taken Perón down a notch, but anyone with half a brain knew he was still a threat. If Argentina was to be saved from a takeover by that fascist, Evita would have to be taken out of the picture.

"Oh my God," Luz shouted into Pilar's ear, barely audible over the applause of the people around them. "We have to get out of here."

"Did you see him?" Pilar shouted in return.

Luz nodded her head and pulled on Pilar's arm. They could hardly move. Pilar pushed and elbowed until they got free of the crush of people. She looked over her shoulder. "I think we have gotten away from him."

"No. No. I still see him." Luz's voice was filled with terror.

Pilar could not see Luz's father anywhere near them, but she sped away with Luz, across to Bolívar, through a knot of celebrating unionists, and around the corner. They crossed the avenida to where Perú became Calle Florida, both of them instinctively making for the safest place either of them knew, the shop where they worked.

Pilar paused in the doorway of a lingerie store and peered behind them. The streets here were nearly empty, though on a Wednesday afternoon in spring, at the hour of the promenade, the outdoor cafés should have been noisy with the chatter of *porteños* comparing plans for next weekend. Instead, the chairs were stacked and the striped umbrellas folded. Three blocks behind the fleeing young women, the crowd at the rally was beginning to break up.

"I think we are safe," Pilar said.

Luz still looked frightened.

Pilar pulled her toward the tearoom across from Harrods department store, a block before Chez Claudia.

"I can't afford to eat here," Luz said.

"We'll just have a cup of English tea. I'll pay." Pilar could not stand the tension. At least if they were in a place with other people, Garmendia would not have the nerve to attack them as he had promised he would when he accosted her in the tango club.

Pilar chose a table near the window so they could watch the street. The waitress eyed Luz as if she recognized her when they ordered their tea. Luz gave her an approving smile as if she were the real Evita. "One day I will buy you a hot chocolate and some cinnamon doughnuts," she whispered to Pilar as soon as the waitress walked away.

In the street outside, the overcast day had turned black: one of those sudden spring tempests was about to descend. Luz soon became distracted by her reflection in the darkened window. As she finished her tea and Pilar counted out the change to pay, Luz said, "Are you going to the club to dance tonight? I want to come with you."

Pilar was incredulous. "Are you crazy? If he saw you with me at the rally, that is the first place he will look for you. I told you he came there trying to find you. I told you what he said."

Luz finally looked away from her reflection. "Who are you talking about?"

"Your father. You said you saw him in the crowd. He could be following us."

"I didn't see my father. I saw Lázaro." She looked disbelieving. "It wasn't my father. It was Lázaro. Torres." Her voice was insistent, as if Pilar didn't know the difference between Luz's father and her ex-boyfriend.

"I thought you said Lázaro was twenty-eight and handsome."

"He is. You said you saw him."

"I didn't," Pilar said. "I saw your father. Not just now. I saw him before, when we got off the Subte, as we came up the steps. He was ahead of us."

"I don't think it was my father. He wouldn't go to a rally like that. He doesn't care about politics. But I saw Lázaro. I know I did."

"Did he see you?"

"I'm not sure, but that's why I ran away."

"Oh my god. This is really dangerous." Pilar could not imagine how bad it would be if both men found them.

Luz looked back at her dark image in the window. "Maybe not. I don't think Lázaro would recognize me. He would think I was her." She said the last word as if it were a prayer.

Pilar swallowed hard. "Let's go to the shop before someone finds us." She watched the street as they walked the last block, and she kept them on the narrow sidewalk, near the buildings, until they got to the front door. The shutters were closed. She used her key to unlock them, put them up, and opened the inner door with the same key.

Once they were inside, the rain came down in torrents. Pilar relocked the door. They went through the heavy green-velvet drapery to the back and sat in the chairs they used during work hours, Pilar behind her sewing machine, Luz next to her ironing board. Pilar stole out to the dark front door from time to time to see if there was anyone outside. Once the rain stopped, a few people went by, some of them carrying placards she had seen at the rally. She wanted to get to the club. To-night was a special performance and a dance competition. She had promised Mariano that she would dance with him.

Luz primped at the mirror and whined that Pilar would not take her to club. "Look how nice my hair looks like this. I want to go." The style was very like what Evita herself had worn that day, upswept in front, hanging down in waves in the back.

Pilar stood her ground. "It is just too dangerous. You have to go home and stay there." Luz made a face but did not argue.

When Pilar went to the front door to leave, she saw a man standing in the doorway of the shoe shop across the street. He glanced at her through the glass of the door and quickly looked away. He could have stopped there just to get out of the rain, but the downpour had let up twenty minutes ago. She went back to Luz, who was rummaging around in the scrap bin, pulling out white tulle.

"Listen," Pilar said, "I don't think you should go out the front when you leave. There's a guy out there."

Luz looked startled. "My father? Lázaro?"

Pilar shook her head. "It wasn't your father, and I don't think it was Lázaro, either. I didn't see this man that well, but he was not like you described Torres."

Luz was twisting the tulle into a ball around her fingers.

Pilar tapped her on the forearm. "Listen! Whoever he is could be watching the store for your father or Lázaro. I am going out through the alley. You'd better, too. Go now and lower the shutter and lock up the front." She gave Luz her key.

Luz said, "Okay," but she continued to sort through the pieces of fabric.

"Promise," Pilar insisted.

"Yes. Yes. I promise. I promise. Stop nagging me."

"Okay. See you tomorrow."

Pilar went to the back door, which opened onto an alley that ran behind the shops. The walkway was narrow and empty except for mops and buckets and trash barrels that the shop owners stowed outside their back doors. Pilar made her way to the end of the block and out onto the *avenida* toward the Subte and the club.

When Juan Perón left the rally with his closest allies in the unions, he went, wearing his tie and jacket, to an early supper at the Plaza Hotel. He was aware that not all the labor representatives supported him, but those eating steaks and potatoes with him in the sumptuously appointed private room knew which side their bread was buttered on. Every one of his companions urged him to do anything he could to restore himself to power.

Evita had gone straight home in the Packard. Alone with only the housekeeper, she listened to radio reports of packs of student protestors along the avenues shouting threats against Perón. "Epithets are also being hurled against the actress Eva Duarte," the announcer reported. His voice was almost gleeful.

———

After Pilar left the shop, Luz stayed in the workroom, playing with fabric from the scrap bin, trying to fashion a hat
like the dramatic white one with beautiful cabbage roses
that she had seen on Evita the day the actress gave her this
beautiful green dress. Pilar and Señora Claudia had said
Evita's white hat was ridiculous, like something from a lamp
store. But to Luz, Evita looked like an English princess in it.
Luz wanted to make such a hat for herself so that she could
look like a princess, too. If Pilar had stayed she might have
been able to show Luz how to do it. She always bragged about
being a seamstress, even said that Evita's mother had been a
seamstress, too. But Pilar was taller and her body rounder.
No one would ever mistake Pilar for the loveliest woman in
Buenos Aires.

Luz pulled the stitches out of her failed attempt at a hat
and touched up her hair and makeup. She took the key. Pilar
had made her swear she would lock up the store and leave by
the alley. Pilar always treated her as if she were an idiot.

She looked out into the alley. It was dark and creepy out
there. Across from their back door was a boarded-up window covered with cobwebs. The air smelled of rotted leaves
and mold. She was more afraid of that ugly place than of
the elegant street out front. She knew how to be careful.
She locked the alley exit.

She returned the scraps to the bin, checked to make
sure the light in the bathroom was out. She even closed the

workroom door before she went out through the dark show-room. She looked out through the glass in the front door. The doorway of the shoe store across the street was empty. The Boston, the coffee bar next to it, was closed, but its name in green neon glowed over its entrance. There was no one out there. Whoever Pilar had seen was gone.

Luz went out and carefully locked the front door. She was about to lower the shutter when someone came up behind her. She did not have time to turn or to scream before he put his hand over her mouth. She froze with fear.

A knife went into the middle of her back. She had lost all sensation before the assailant made five more cuts and left her bleeding in the doorway of the shop.

At that very moment, Detective Roberto Leary of the Federal Police was in the Palermo district, waiting in the parlor of an aristocratic Italianate villa to speak with a witness to a murder. The room Leary stood in, holding his fedora in his hands, was furnished with French antiques—lots of small chairs with delicate curved legs and seats of needlepoint, but not like the bright cushions his mother and older sister made. These had tiny stitches and subtle colors that matched the flower-patterned carpet beneath his shoes. The walls were hung with paintings of landscapes in heavy, gold-leafed frames.

Leary knew he did not belong in a place like this, but he did not belong in his job, either. He used to. Not anymore. With the help of his father's brother, he had enthusiastically joined the Capital Police seven years ago, right after he left secondary school. In those days he was glad to have had a job at all, and one he thought he wanted at that. His first years on the force were pretty much what he had hoped: a completely masculine endeavor, unlike being in the house where he had grown up, after his father's death, with all women—his mother, his grandmother, and his three sisters. During his first several years on the force, he had patrolled the barrios of his beautiful city. He picked up insolent *compadritos* with their fancy shoes and switchblades and rid Buenos Aires of thugs and jerks who plagued the neighborhoods. He had liked that a lot. Once he was promoted to detective, he grew to love his job.

But that was before the Capitals were merged into the federal force at the beginning of this year. Since the Federals had taken over, Leary's motivation had waned, until now it was practically nonexistent. The job he used to do, the job he still wanted, was gone. Instead, his work had become more about politics than crime. This murder was a perfect example of the kind of sham investigation he spent his time on looking into the death of a student in an antigovernment demonstration. Ordinarily, such an event would have gotten less than lip service; except in this case, his captain owed the dead kid's grandfather a big favor. The old guy was a bigwig demanding an investigation. As far as Leary's chief was concerned, Leary was an underdog, first of all because he had come from the Capitals, which the higher-ups, all ex-Federals, considered a bunch of pussies. And he had another strike against him. His uncle, who had pulled strings to get him the job in the first place, had died. Now Leary had no godfather with clout to defend his interests. So he had to do the dirty work and smile, and today that meant pretending to find out who had killed the kid. He would have liked to go after the murderer for real, but the student had died while demonstrating against Perón, and Police Chief Velasco was beholden to Juan Perón for his position. Figuring out how far his boss expected him to go with this investigation was harder than solving any crime. Guessing was an ex-Capital cop's only alternative. Right now Velasco's own position was tenuous. The big boss's own ass might end up in a sling. The scuttlebutt was that Perón himself was about to be arrested—to get him permanently out of the way. Would Velasco throw his own *patron* in the pokey? There was always a chance Velasco would get tossed out of office on the heels of the departing colonel. That was a lot to hope for. Most of the men on the force supported Perón because he was a supporter of the hardworking poor. Leary liked that, too, so he guessed he liked Perón. Sort of. But that bastard Velasco was a different question entirely. Leary couldn't find anything to like about him.

Leary was determined to keep his job, so for now his best bet was to make a show of solving this case, but not to try too hard.

The dead student, Alberto Ara, had lived in this palace. His ilk had long-since abandoned their educational opportunities for the chance to shout anti-Perón sentiments in the streets. The kids were demanding a return to the nation's constitution. If Leary thought about it, that was what he wanted, too. That kind of move would force the cops to stop being political and solve real crimes. Which was what Leary wanted to do, instead of working for a political hack who didn't give a rat's ass who had killed the boy.

He glanced at his Bulova watch—like his job and his car, a gift from his dead uncle. It was going on eight o'clock, and he hadn't eaten since noon. He was trying to figure out how much longer to wait when a door in the room's walnut paneling opened and a guy of about twenty-three walked in. Leary caught a glimpse of a weeping woman in the hall before the door closed on her hurt, inquiring glance.

"Who are you and what do you want?" the youth demanded without preamble. He was a slender, good-looking boy, a couple of inches taller than Leary. His dark, perfectly tailored suit cost five times as much as any young detective's.

Leary shifted his fedora to his left hand and extended his right. The youth did not take it. Leary shrugged and said only, "Inspector Roberto Leary." He could no longer say "of the Capital Police," and he wouldn't say, "of the Federals," because they were known throughout the land as a bunch of heartless thugs.

"I am Eduardo Ara," the young man said. "The maid said you were here about my brother's murder." He looked something between grieved and peeved.

"Yes," Leary said. "I am supposed to be investigating who killed your brother. I am sorry to have pulled you away from your family at this moment."

"But you have, haven't you?" His sneer made Leary want to paste him one. This rich boy was obviously not accustomed to being polite to someone as lowly as a policeman.

"I just want to ask you a few questions, to see if I can get a lead as to who might have . . ." Leary left the rest of his thought unstated. He pointed to a stiff settee that looked as if it would be only slightly less uncomfortable than continuing to stand, but before he could ask to sit down, the kid shook his head.

"I am getting ready to take my mother and my grandmother to the country now that that travesty of a funeral is over. It was a circus, you know. Cops on horseback, treating me and the other students like we were criminals."

"I'm sorry," Leary said, trying to get the kid to soften up and give him information. "I'll try to be brief as possible. What can you tell me about the circumstances of your brother's death?"

"Alberto and I are . . . were students together," Eduardo Ara said. "He was two years younger than me. We were in a group of other students demonstrating for a return to constitutional government. We were entirely within our rights. We have to stand up for what we believe."

Leary smiled without really agreeing. This elegantly dressed, pomaded scion of the upper classes was not exactly the type one would find rabble-rousing in the streets in an ordinary city. But Buenos Aires was not ordinary, and neither were the *porteños*, her citizens. Everyone and everything in this cosmopolitan capital gave the impression of being misplaced, as if a piece of Spain or Italy had been torn off from the little continent north across the water and stuck here on the edge of a vast wild land of Indians and desolation. Argentine kids, like this one, seemed to have no idea how many young men their age had been slaughtered fighting a war all over the world in the past few years, while here they safely ate steaks, pretended to study architecture or literature, and tried to seduce one another's sisters.

Ara's sneer deepened into disdain. "Those repressive goons who attacked our group were probably members of your police department. How am I supposed to believe that you will honestly try to find my brother's murderer?"

Leary hated it that the young snob was probably right. He chose to ignore the remark altogether. "Before you leave town, what can you tell me that would help my investigation? I want to try to catch the people who murdered Alberto. At the very least, it will comfort your grandfather to know his grandson's death did not go ignored."

The kid began to inch his way to the door. At that rate, it would take him several minutes to get there. This baronial parlor was three times the size of Leary's whole apartment.

"My grandfather is dreaming," Ara said. "There is no way anyone will ever be accused, much less punished, for what happened. Stop acting like anyone in the government gives a shit about one more dead student."

Leary touched Ara's shoulder, stopping him from continuing to the door. "The fastest way to get rid of me would be to tell me what you know."

Ara looked unconvinced, but he answered. "There is nothing to say. We were marching to demand the rule of law. A car went past, its horn screeching. A guy in it stuck the nose of a machine gun out the window and fired into the crowd. Alberto took a volley." He looked as if he would burst into tears.

Leary waited for him to regain control. He took his notebook from his jacket pocket. "Can you give me any detail that might identify the car?"

The boy shook his head. "I was busy diving out of its way. It was dark green." His face turned defiant. "A military color, I believe." He strode to the door and opened it.

Leary saw that the kid felt guilty that he had saved himself and not his brother. He put his fedora back on his head. "I am sorry for your loss," he said. "Take care of your family." He didn't wait for Eduardo to see him out but marched past him to the villa's front door and got out of there as fast as he could.

He drove back to police headquarters, writing his useless report in his head on his way. He was barely through the front door when his captain intercepted him and handed him a slip of paper with an address on Florida Street. "A woman—stabbed to death in front of a *modista*'s shop. A patrol car is already there," was all he said.

Leary looked at the address and then up at his boss's retreating back. He was not going to get any help from that self-centered son of a bitch. Nor anything to eat for the next couple of hours. He shoved the paper into his pocket, made an about-face, and went back to the parking lot. This was a strange call. Violence was prevalent these days, but most of it was political—like the death of the Ara boy. Streetwalkers might catch hell; they always did, but they would not be hanging around at a place like that. Florida was a street where pickpockets roamed, especially at crowded times like Easter and Christmas, but the switchblade wielders who plagued the rest of the city rarely, if ever, intruded there. Leary had never heard of a woman killed with a knife on the most exclusive shopping street in town.

He drove his dead uncle's classy red Pontiac to the scene of the crime. With the traffic sparse and the center deserted, it took him less than twenty minutes. He passed the opulent Galerías Pacifico—a four-story crystal palace of expensive stores and marble coffee bars. Flood lamps here and there on balconies lit up sections of the brown stone facade, but the manikins in the windows stood in the dark, so no one could see how grand they looked in their silk suits and slinky cruise wear. The usual shoppers, diners, moviegoers from among the idle rich who might have jammed the pedestrian area roundabout were absent thanks to the early-evening storms and the turbulent times.

Leary's tires rumbled over the cobblestones as he turned from Córdoba onto Florida. He wondered what it would be like to have nothing to do but play polo and look for the latest fashions. The car he drove was the only stylish thing he was ever likely to own, inherited from his father's brother who had made good in the U.S.A. and had come home just in time to die. The Pontiac was beautiful and purred to Leary as it glided down the narrow *calle*.

Cast-iron streetlamps spilled pools of light at intervals along the empty walkway in front of shuttered shop windows. The rain had left puddles that glistened in his headlights. The patrol car he was looking for was stopped on the narrow sidewalk halfway between Corrientes and Sarmiento. Its high beams shone into the doorway of a dress shop. Leary scrunched his whitewall tires against the curb as he pulled up behind the other car.

As soon as he got out, he saw the victim. Oh, shit. The body lying in the entryway was a girl's, small and slender. Very young. Bad enough to be on permanent night shift when it meant investigating carved-up *compadritos* killed in their petty gangster knife fights. But a dead teenage girl? Younger than his youngest sister? Shit. Shit.

"Hola, muchachos," he called without enthusiasm to the uniformed men standing over the body. They parted, revealing the girl's head. Disbelief stopped him in his tracks. It could not be. The dead person was the actress Eva Duarte? The mistress of the just deposed vice president of Argentina? And the captain had sent him to investigate? Velasco had not come himself? A murder like this should have brought out the minister of justice, if there was one after the government housecleaning of the past twenty-four hours. Maybe Velasco himself had already been thrown out—creature of Perón that he was.

"I don't think it's her," Ireno Estrada said. He was short and muscular and never kept his shirt collar buttoned once he left the station. Of all the nephews of minor-league politicians on the force, he at least had a brain in his head.

Leary pushed back his fedora and leaned over the body. "She could have fooled me." On closer inspection, the nose, the mouth did not look exactly like the face on the covers of his mother's soap opera fan magazines, but everything else . . . "Was she on her back like this when you found her?"

"No. I turned her over to make sure she was dead." This was from Estrada's chubby partner—Rodolfo Franco, whose mother's second husband had the contract to pick up garbage in the Palermo district. The well-to-do refuse collector had dumped this particular piece of low-wattage trash on the Buenos Aires Municipal Police Force. Anyone with two centavos' worth of brain cells would have concluded, from the size of the pool of blood surrounding the body, that there was not enough left in the poor girl to keep a mosquito alive.

Her dress, where it was not soaked with blood, was pale green and looked expensive. A small, cheap purse on a metal-chain handle hung from her forearm. The real Evita Duarte, he was sure, would not have been caught dead in these tacky stiletto-heeled patent-leather shoes, one of which was half off the dead girl's foot. But this waif had been caught dead in them. Where would a girl who could not afford decent shoes have gotten this dress?

He reached up and closed her eyes, then opened her purse. It seemed almost as much of an invasion as the knife had made. He took out a small glassine envelope with her identity card and held it up to the beam of the patrol car's headlights. "Luz Garmendia. It says she lives on Colombres. She was sixteen." His voice choked on the last word.

There was one peso, sixty-nine centavos in the purse, and a handkerchief edged with the kind of lace working-class girls made with fine cotton. Then, he noticed a glint of metal at the margin of the pool of blood, near the girl's right hand. "A key." This was odd. Poor girls did not live in houses that were ever locked. "The dress is too expensive for the shoes and purse." He was thinking out loud.

Franco guffawed. His soft belly wobbled when he laughed. "Big expert in girls' dresses, are you, Robo?"

Leary would gladly have strangled the knucklehead. "I have three sisters," he said instead of a curse. He had been warned too often that his arrogance toward the politically well connected was not a proper path to promotion on the force. "I don't imagine you know anything at all about women."

An ambulance siren approached from the north. Leary got to his feet and on a whim tried the key in the lock of the shop door. It opened. He looked up at the sign across the top of the entrance. CHEZ CLAUDIA, it said in large gold letters, and under it in elegant script, *STYLE POUR LES FEMMES*.

"Reno, find out where the owner of this shop lives and get me a phone number for him." The ambulance pulled up. The spinning red light reflected off the girl's blood.

The driver approached with a stretcher. One glance and he looked stunned. "Holy God!"

"It's not her," Leary said. But a suspicion was beginning to form in his mind that whoever had stabbed this poor girl had made the same mistake.

All over Buenos Aires at that moment people were worried, angry, puzzled. In their hovels in the *villas miserias* around the factories on the periphery, the poor rejoiced over the parting gifts Perón had announced over the radio in his farewell speech, but even more, they feared that his fall from power would take away the gains they had won from his hands.

In posh apartments overlooking lush parks, or on patios with views of star-filled skies, and in the mahogany-paneled bar at the Officer's Club in the Palacio Paz, the rich and the powerful told one another of their outrage over Perón's audacity. They despised his final attempt to buy off the trash who did the dirtiest jobs in the land. More than a few of them believed Perón's mistress was behind his outrageous behavior. They condemned "that woman" as the greatest threat to their society. Much as they hated Perón, it was the avaricious actress they cursed. It terrified them to think Evita, the venal and social-climbing virago, would resurrect her lover and rob them of their lifestyles of luxury. The words of the tango told them: the guilty are always the women. More than one self-satisfied plutocrat let out a dirty guffaw when he pointed out that like the woman who had committed mankind's original sin, this viperous temptress was called Eva.

It was well after midnight before the millionaire denizens of the Jockey Club or the Círculo des Armas turned their minds toward practical ways in which they might avoid a calamitous uprising incited by Señorita Duarte.

Meanwhile, the actress was, from the start, all practicality. Before darkness fell, she sent Jorge and Cristina to the Brazilian grocery on the next block to buy canned foods that could sustain them if they were forced to endure a siege. She filled the bathtubs with water, in case the officials decided to cut them off from the necessities of life. She packed suitcases for a quick getaway and considered sewing her jewels into the hems of her skirts.

Perón took a soldier's precautions, closing and locking the shutters, checking and loading his pistol, and posting three sergeants armed with machine guns at his apartment door.

THURSDAY, OCTOBER 11

In the wee hours of the next morning, Rudi Freude, the son of a German immigrant billionaire and, some say, Nazi spy, who had been hard at work arranging for the importation of German gold and brainpower, drove a Benz touring car to the servants' entrance of the massive, elegant apartment building where Perón and Evita had enjoyed their illegitimate cohabitation. Unnoticed by the crowd watching the front door, the little lady and her lover and a couple of small suitcases were swept away to Tres Bocas, a remote retreat where the bluebloods from the Avenida Alvear kept enormous country "cottages," and where Evita and Juan could secret themselves in the home of a supporter. Domingo Mercante, Perón's most trusted adviser, accompanied them.

The Benz arrived at a dock where the boats of the wealthy awaited summer, when they would take their owners along tree-lined channels to their peaceful getaways. Once the fugitives had boarded one of them, Freude wrapped Evita in a blanket for the chilly ride.

Subdued and worried, Perón sat in the stern of the boat and whispered with Mercante. Evita pulled the blanket around her like a shawl and stood at the railing. In the moonlight, the water was the color of pewter and looked solid enough to walk on.

Freude tried his best to cheer her, plying her with hot coffee from a thermos and pointing out huge villas where, in the gardens, white blossoms of spring fluoresced in the midnight moonbeams. "I was at a party in that one," he said of a two-story mansion, still boarded up and awaiting the vacation season. "It belongs to a friend of my father's named Wagener. They have a great art collection, including a beautiful portrait by an artist named Klimt. I wish I could show it to you."

Evita wondered how he could think about pictures under the circumstances. She glanced back at Perón, hunched over, his hand cupped, lighting one cigarette from another. "I wish we were on a boat to Paris," she said.

Rudi gave her a doubtful smile. "Beautiful place," he said. "I was there often after we took it in forty-three. I am sure you will see it one day."

She fell silent. A dull, cloudy Thursday was dawning by the time they finally arrived at the safe house. It looked more like a Black Forest chalet than an Argentine hideaway.

Once Perón and Evita were delivered, Freude and the loyal Mercante took their leave.

Perón put his arm around Evita as they waved good-bye until the boat disappeared into the gray gloom that smelled of mud. Perón spoke German to the caretaker, who built them a fire in the fireplace, brewed them some coffee, and trundled off to his apartment over the stable.

They sat close together on a soft sofa before the fire. "Is Mercante going to get the union leaders to stand up for you?" she asked him.

"He says he will do everything humanly possible to reverse the events of the past few days, but it's a tricky business," Perón responded.

"You will need all your strength to fight those lily-livered idiots. If you show them any weakness they will eat you alive." She delivered the line as if it were from one of her scripts when she had played Catherine the Great and Queen Elizabeth on the radio. For a moment she had an eerie feeling that her real life was being created by a scriptwriter for a radio drama. She squeezed his hand. She wondered if she would ever be an actress on the radio again. That bastard Yankelevich had called her and summarily fired her from Radio Belgrano the second Perón resigned. But she did not speak of this. Perón was too discouraged already. She snuggled closer to him.

His sigh seemed forced, like that of an actor trying to make it heard over the airwaves. "I have warned Domingo to cooperate with the Federal Police if they come looking for us."

"If?" she asked, in a voice uncharacteristically satiric, completely atypical of her way with her colonel. "Is there any doubt that the officers and the ruling class will do whatever they can to stop you from helping the poor? And without Velasco in charge, they now have the police in their pockets."

At almost that very second, a member of the police force that Evita so feared telephoned Perón's apartment on the Calle Posadas and spoke to Jorge Webber, the chauffeur, who had been left to hold down the fort. Roberto Leary was glad to hear that the actress had gone out of town in the middle of the night to a secret hideout over a hundred kilometers from the city. If there was a madman out to kill her, at least she was safely in hiding. Leary gave Perón's man his phone number and extracted a promise that Webber would call him if the actress returned to Buenos Aires.

Leary inhaled deeply to steel his nerves. This first task had turned out to be easy. His next job would, he was sure, be extremely unpleasant. He dialed the phone number of Claudia Robles, the *modista* who owned the shop where Luz Garmendia had been stabbed to death.

At ten that morning, Hernán Mantell drove Claudia Robles to meet a policeman at her shop. Hernán was at war with himself. With the latest upheaval, the government could totter either way. The journalist in him hoped for a return to the democratic constitution, which had been largely ignored for decades and then totally suspended when the military took over the government two years earlier.

At that point, citizens' rights went out the window. The newspapers had been censored, but now Perón's departure left only the indecisive Fárrell in charge and the army with only a tenuous hold on power. If the future tipped in the direction Hernán hoped for, freedom of the press might be restored.

Hernán's editor had called him at seven thirty to tell him that General Avalos was taking over as minister of war, which could mean only that Perón's ouster was complete. Still, the army had almost no support among the people—less actually without Perón, since he at least had his *descamisados* down in the factories on the periphery. At this point, matters could open up or descend into even greater repression. And what of Perón? He didn't seem the type to go quietly into that good night.

Hernán's work, even his existence, hung in the balance, but whatever his anxieties for his own future, the horrible news that had come just before dawn—of the murder of the girl Luz—had torn his mind away from those worries. How could he leave Claudia, his wife in all but name?

He had had a lawful wife when he was barely out of his teens, a willing girl who had seemed almost as desperate for sex as he had been. When they were discovered together in the backseat of her father's car parked in the family garage, he had been forced to marry her. Nothing much had happened between them after that. She repented her wanton ways, and as quick as she had been to open her legs before

marriage, she kept them firmly closed after the hastily arranged ceremony. They grew apart, had not seen each other
for decades, but he could not marry Claudia—the love of his
life—because there was no divorce in Catholic Argentina.

Duty called him to work, but love kept him with Claudia,
at least until he delivered her into the arms of her father. The
old man had taken the Subte to arrive at the shop on Florida
at nine. By the time Hernán drove Claudia there, Gregorio
Robles probably would have broken the news to Pilar, the
seamstress. Having lovingly raised his daughter by himself,
Gregorio would know how to comfort the young Pilar. He
would also be there to greet the detective who was coming
to interview Claudia about the murder. That is, if the policeman arrived early. Devotion to duty was not a signature habit
of the Buenos Aires police force.

One of Hernán's biggest worries was what Claudia and
her father would say to the investigator. Some people were
taking the recent relaxation of the state of siege as a signal
that the citizenry was safe from repression. But Hernán knew
that if Claudia or old Gregorio said anything too controver-
sial, they would wind up on somebody's list of subversives.

When Claudia got into the car, she saw the worry in
Hernán's glance and mistook it for annoyance. He was getting
fed up with her uncontrolled outpouring of grief. She did not
want to irritate him further, but she wound up spending the
entire ride from their apartment to her shop recounting her
relationship with the dead child: a story Hernán knew, but
that she could not stop herself from repeating. "I thought

I was helping her," she said for the tenth time that morning. She stared out the window and relived the shock and disbelief of receiving the horrendous news that had come before the break of light.

A telephone call at that hour never brings good tidings. When they jumped out of bed and ran for the phone in the parlor, they both had imagined the call would be for him. Some political crisis required coverage—there had certainly been enough of that lately. She let him pick it up. When he said, "It's for you," and handed her the phone, she could not imagine who it was. Her father lived in a small apartment on the floor just below them. It could not be him. He did not have a phone. The shop? A fire? But it was worse. So terribly worse. Neither of them had slept for the rest of the night.

Sitting in the car, she rubbed her eyes with her soaked linen handkerchief and again went over the day, a little more than six months ago, when she had taken Luz Garmendia under her wing.

Almost daily, from the window of her third-floor apartment she had seen the tiny and timid girl of fifteen bringing lunch to that brute of a gardener, her lover Lázaro Torres. He repeatedly abused the child, spitting on the food she had prepared, calling it shit, and flinging it in her face. If he did such nasty things in public, Claudia did not even want to imagine what he did to her in private.

She had discussed Torres's behavior with her father, who then wanted to talk to the gardener. She could not allow that. The frail old man was no match for the muscular Torres.

Gregorio had told her what the neighbors were saying: that the girl Luz had run away from a brutal father. "This is the problem of parents being unkind to children," her father had said. "The children get used to it and expect to be abused all their lives. They never learn to stand up for themselves."

Out of fear, Claudia had kept her peace with the situation until she could no longer stand the thought of the girl's suffering. One day, she decided she must intervene. She waited at home until noontime, watching out the window until Luz approached, delivering her lover's lunch. Claudia quickly went down the stairs as if she were in hurry to get to work and secretly handed Luz a slip of paper as she passed the girl on the sidewalk in front of the building. She did not look back, but she heard the child presenting her bastard boyfriend with another disdained lunch. Later that day, Luz called the number on the paper. Claudia invited her to the shop, gave her a job, and found her a decent place to live. She had felt so happy with herself, so self-satisfied that she had rescued the girl. Now Luz was dead, and Claudia was certain that if she had let the girl be, she might still be alive. She also knew it was probably Lázaro Torres who had killed her.

As Hernán pulled his old Ford coupe up to the curb in front of the shop, he took her hand and kissed her damp palm before she got out of the car. "I'll try not to be too late," he said. "When my editor called this morning, he told me Perón has left town. If he just keeps going, it could be the end of him, but the situation is heating up in other ways. I promise I'll do my best."

She leaned across the seat and kissed him. The apology in his eyes told her clearly what his words belied, that the political events would keep him from her on the day she needed him most. But she knew that *La Prensa,* his newspaper, would be one of the first to be suppressed if events turned out the way his worst nightmares warned him they might. And the facts of Argentina's past and present told them both that they probably would. She was as passionate about her work as he was about his, but his was serious. She made expensive dresses; he reported and recorded events that would become history. He loved her. She knew he did. But he was going to do his duty and leave her with her grief.

She touched his face and slipped out of the car. "Phone me at the paper," he called out the window as she crossed the narrow cement sidewalk. A glance at the tiles in the shop's doorway turned her stomach. She ran though the showroom, past a strange man who stood with her father in the workroom, and into the bathroom in the rear of the store. She slammed the door behind her and vomited into the toilet.

The small tiles in front had been just like these on the floor of this bathroom, small black-and-white hexagons. But those at the front door were now a pinkish brown. Luz's blood, the blood of that poor dead child, had been cleaned away by she knew not whom, but the stain of death remained on her doorstep. She retched again and did not stop until her stomach was completely empty.

She rinsed her mouth and looked at her face in the mirror, so pale she hardly recognized her own withdrawn, shocked countenance. She took a compact from her purse and patted a useless layer of pressed powder onto the dark streaks under her eyes, left by sleeplessness and guilt.

She took off her hat, fluffed her hair out of habit, and unwound her long gray silk scarf from her neck. In the workroom, she held out her hand to the stocky, fit-looking man in the dark pin-striped suit standing next to her father. He was, as she knew he must be, the detective who had called and described the dead girl. He must also have been up all night, but unlike her looked only a little the worse for wear. Then again, he was younger than she, by close to twenty years, she guessed. "I am so sorry for your trouble," he said. "My name is Roberto Leary." She saw the Irish in his good looks and the Latin in his sad, dark eyes.

Her father kissed her and held her hand. "I looked at his credentials," he said. "They are in order."

"Has Pilar arrived?" she asked her father.

"She called to say she would be a little late." He looked at his watch. "She will be here in a few minutes."

"Papa, would you go across to the Boston and ask them to bring us a tray of coffees? Get one for Pilar, too."

When her father had gone, she and the detective pulled up chairs around the high cutting table. Leary put his brown fedora under his seat and took out a notepad. "I am afraid I have to ask you a lot of questions," he said.

"Yes, I imagined you would. I have been thinking about her since you called and how this could have happened."

"I have, too," Leary said to the proprietress of Chez Claudia. She was, as he had expected, an elegant woman: early, maybe middle forties, but still statuesque and vital, though obviously exhausted. He started as he always did with witnesses, by asking a few lead-up questions about how long she had owned the shop and where she lived—meant just to get her used to answering his inquiries. She had started to tell him how Luz Garmendia came to be working for her when a fine-featured girl of about twenty or so came in through the back door from the alley behind the stores. She was sleek and curvaceous, but she also looked shocked and tired. Her eyes were as red as her lipstick.

"This is Pilar Borelli," Claudia Robles said. "She is my seamstress. I called her early this morning and told her the terrible news." The girl put her hat and jacket on a clothes tree near the back door and took a chair without saying a word.

"I am sorry for your loss," Leary said. He offered her his hand, which she took for only a second. "From all I have been able to find out in the house where Luz Garmendia lived, you two were probably the ones who knew the dead girl best."

"If you don't count her father and her ex-lover," Señora Robles said.

"We have not been able to locate them yet. We talked to her grandmother early this morning. She identified the body," he said. He did not tell them that the old lady had never dropped a tear or shown even a hint of grief. "Evidently Torres, her former boyfriend, and her father both have the habit of going on benders, even on a Wednesday.

But my men will find them." He said the last with more confidence than he felt. The frequent demonstrations for or against Perón, and the underworld activity, which always spiked during moments of instability, would take all attention away from this investigation into the murder, however brutal, of an obscure girl. Only a police-force outsider such as himself could be spared for this unimportant task. He had played the only card he had to get this overtime approved— that the murderer probably had been after the actress Eva Duarte.

Claudia continued answering his rather innocuous questions until her father came back, followed by a waiter from the café carrying a tray of demitasse cups and a sugar bowl. Once the waiter left, Leary downed a coffee and opened his notepad. He watched Pilar put two spoons of sugar into her cup and stir and stir. He shook his attention from the mesmerizing motion of the seamstress's hand twirling the spoon and proceeded to ask them to tell him about the dead girl and her habits. Like most witnesses, they also told him who they thought might have killed the girl. The reasons were all emotional, of course, but they fit with the facts of this case. Six stab wounds were too many for a simple robbery or a coldhearted assassination.

Claudia watched the detective scrawl his notes with his stub of a pencil that looked as if it had been sharpened with a penknife. She lit a cigarette and only half listened to Pilar tell him about her friendship with Luz. The seamstress described the dead girl as an innocent, which was accurate despite what moralizers about female virtue might think of a girl still in her teens who ran away with a man nearly twice her age.

Claudia smashed out her cigarette in the ashtray next to her empty coffee cup and looked down at the sketch pad in front of her. While Pilar was giving her evidence to the pleasant-faced policeman, Claudia the *modista* had absent-mindedly drawn a design for widow's weeds. She put down her pencil.

Leary looked up from his notes. "Don't you think it's possible," he asked, "that whoever killed Luz did it because he mistook her for Evita Duarte?"

Claudia shuddered. If that was true, she was doubly guilty for having connected the impressionable girl with the actress in the first place. Leary proceeded to ask Pilar a lot of questions about Luz's desire to be mistaken for the actress and the green dress she had on when she died.

Guilt washed over Claudia again. Less than a week ago she had caught Luz, right here in the shop, in her attempt to remake herself into the actress. Claudia had been in a hurry to get everything ready for her best customer's fitting that morning. Evita had ordered a special outfit to wear for Juan Perón's fiftieth-birthday lunch, and Claudia had designed a lovely ensemble of dark red with white polka dots—gorgeous Italian silk that complemented Evita's perfect, pale skin. Claudia had arrived at the shop early that sunny morning to check over the dress and also a matching set of beige satin shirt and trousers. Evita had been expected at ten thirty.

Claudia had entered from the bright street and her eyes had a hard time adjusting. She had thought she saw Evita already there an hour before she was expected, admiring herself in the triple mirror. Claudia rubbed her eyes and looked again at the figure in slacks and shirt.

The woman on the beige-carpeted pedestal turned and faced her. It was Luz, her shop assistant, not her best customer. Until last Saturday, even from the rear Luz's brown hair would have given her away.

The startled girl shouted, "Señora Robles!"

"What are you doing sporting that hairdo?" Claudia had demanded. Luz's now-blond hair and its style and her makeup as well mimicked the actress's. With that hairdo, those arched eyebrows, and that dark red shade of lipstick, clearly the girl wanted to be mistaken for Evita.

On closer inspection, the quality of the dye job was a dead giveaway, as was the lack of subtlety in the application of the eyebrow pencil. Nor did Luz have Evita's large, piercing eyes or delicate nose, and no one else had the actress's luminous complexion. But in Evita's clothing, appearing in this place that Evita frequented, it was easy to mistake Luz for the mistress of Juan Perón.

"I—I—" Luz did not finish the sentence.

Never imagining that a teenage girl playing dress-up could be putting herself in mortal danger, Claudia had done nothing more than point to her watch and warn Luz about the time. "She'll be here in half an hour. Take off those clothes and that makeup and redo your hair. She likes you to model her outfits before she takes them home, but I doubt she will be pleased if she sees you trying to turn yourself into her. Get going."

Luz had stepped down and disappeared into the dressing room. She had greeted the actress that day as a blond, but with her hair pulled back into a tight chignon. If Evita had noticed the change in the girl's hair color, she had not remarked on it. That was the day the actress had given Luz the green dress in which she had met her death, and Claudia knew she herself was to blame.

If this detective's theory was true, Claudia thought, she could have saved Luz's life by making her change her hair back to its natural color and putting a stop to her masquerade. While Leary continued to question Pilar, Claudia looked into her empty coffee cup and forced herself not to light another cigarette. Why hadn't she done more to save that poor child?

Guilt also gnawed at Pilar. She answered the handsome detective's questions and insisted in her heart that it was Luz's father who had killed her.

"If you ask me . . ." she started to say. But she swallowed her words. Who was she to tell a policeman anything? She was afraid of knowing what she did. She did not want to give evidence. In Buenos Aires, people who gave evidence in a killing too often wound up dead themselves. Knowing who had killed Luz would not bring her back.

A fleeting smile brought out the boyishness of Detective Leary's looks, but it quickly disappeared. He regarded her with his policeman's mask. "You were about to say?"

She could not resist the expectation in his eyes. "Her father," she whispered, because she had to say something.

"Her father what?" Leary demanded.

"She was always afraid he would find out where she lived or where she worked. She said he would drag her back home by her hair."

Leary imagined what it would be like to run his fingers through the pretty seamstress's shiny black hair. "You were the last one to see her alive. Did you see anyone in the street that night as you were leaving here?"

He saw fear flash in the girl's dark eyes. She was hiding something, or she was implicated somehow. Those delicate hands that apparently were so skillful in creating outrageously expensive gowns didn't look as if they could have plunged a knife into the body of another human being. He could imagine them guiding silk under the needle of her sewing machine. He could imagine the skin on her arms feeling like the silk she sewed.

He dragged his mind from where it wanted to go and focused on her boss. "Why was the girl dressed up to look like Eva Duarte?" This was the crux of his thinking. He, Franco, and Estrada, even the girl's grandmother looking at her dead body, had at first glance mistaken her for the actress. Perón was the most hated man in Argentina, and though he had already resigned by the time the girl was killed, the murderer may still have been trying to get at the colonel by murdering his mistress.

Leary reminded them of his theory. "What do you think?" he asked them directly. "Could the murderer have mistaken her for the actress? It was not quite dark at the hour when she was killed, but the day was cloudy, and this street is narrow. Is it conceivable that the actress would be here at that hour?"

Señora Robles said, "Yes."

Pilar Borelli said, "No."

Both of them had spoken too quickly and vehemently.

The old man grunted. Leary turned to him. "Who do you think did it?"

"I have no idea, but Perón *has* been the target of all that hatred pouring out in demonstrations." He pointed to the newspaper on the table in front of him. "The public outcry against him has gotten worse in the last month or two. I also hate him, but not for the reason anyone else does." His voice was definite, his face determined.

Gregorio Robles had to be seventy if he was a day. He didn't look like any murderer Leary had ever heard of. "Why do you hate him so much?"

"He went for young girls. I have a daughter. I cannot imagine such a man. His last mistress before Eva Duarte was only fourteen years old. He took her out in public and introduced her as his niece. He disgusts me for that."

The señora and Pilar looked dismayed. Leary couldn't tell if they were shocked by the old man's revelation or by the fact that he had brought it up. Saying such a thing to some policemen could get even a seventy-five-year-old arrested. Leary wasn't that kind of cop. But they didn't know that. He had heard those rumors about Perón. A guy on the force talked about it all the time, made jokes about how only a man with an undersized male member would be a cradle robber. That cop told a story of having been on a detail once, escorting a group of Croatian immigrants from the port to Perón's office. The colonel's little "niece" had been in the minister's outer office, dressed like a schoolgirl, sitting in a big chair where her feet didn't even reach the floor. Of course, that story came out when the higher-ups, all former Federals, were not around. It would not do for any of them to be caught laughing about their ultimate boss being a pervert. Ordinary grunts on the city police force were no safer from the goon squads than were the citizens at large.

Leary let the comment pass. He made a show of writing down the names of the two men they suspected and asking for information about how to find Torres. No one around the table seemed at all impressed with his Evita–look-alike theory.

Pilar Borelli stuck to her guns about Miguel Garmendia. "Her father came to Club Gardel, where I dance," she said, her voice intense and tinged with fear. She described a scene that gave credence to her conviction. The brute had made an out-and-out threat. Considering how cold and uncaring his mother had been on seeing her dead granddaughter and the fact that even she described her son as a hopeless drunk, he was probably more than capable of violence toward Luz.

"Luz told me," Pilar said, "that he beat her all the time, from when she was a very little kid." She made the case against Garmendia even more credible. "That's why she ran away as soon as she was old enough."

Leary, who believed that Luz had never really gotten old enough to run away, looked to Claudia Robles for confirmation, but she shrugged and said, "I know she lived with the gardener who works at my apartment building, a man nearly fifteen years older than she, and he was cruel to her in public. That speaks for how he must have treated her in private." Claudia looked down at her lap. "I thought I was rescuing her from an evil existence by giving her a job and finding her a decent place to live." Tears started to fall from her eyes onto the pad where she had been scribbling most of the time.

"When did Luz come to work here?"

"A little over six months ago."

"And when did she start making herself up to look like Eva Duarte?" Leary asked.

"Just in the last week," Claudia Robles answered. "I gave her a raise. She must have used the money for a dye job." She gave him a hurt look, as if he had forced her to confess to the crime.

He turned to the pretty tango dancer. "When did you encounter her father in the Club Gardel?"

"Only a few days ago."

He closed his notepad. "Perhaps," he said to Pilar, "you should stay away from the club for now, considering that Garmendia knows you go there."

She looked at him as if he had suggested she cut off her leg.

"At the very least," he said, "watch out for him. If he comes anywhere near you, call me." He handed her a card with the phone number of his office. She picked it up with both hands, read it, and then pierced him with a look. Her deep-set, dark almond eyes were inquiring, but there was an undercurrent of fear in her voice when she spoke. "I will," she said. "I will."

Ramón Ybarra, back in uniform and accompanying his commanding officer General Avalos to the Casa Rosada, listened with satisfaction as President Fárrell named his boss to take over one of Perón's posts: minister of war. Progress, at last. Perhaps now Avalos would stop sleepwalking and take steps to prevent any uprising in favor of Perón. The only way to accomplish that would be by force.

"Colonel Perón has left town," Fárrell reported, as if that settled the matter for good. This president had been Perón's creature. In the most recent shake-up, the tall, power-hungry colonel, of too low a rank to take over the presidency himself, had needed a weak superior officer to be the titular head of the government. Perón had put his considerable strength behind Fárrell. A perfect choice for the puppet master. President Fárrell had the personality of a skink. He might kill a fly, but that was about the extent of his combative impulse. But with Avalos as minister of war there was a chance for a show of strength. Avalos commanded the troops at the Campo de Mayo—at least a third, maybe a half of the Argentine army. He could order them into Buenos Aires with a phone call.

"Things will calm down now," Fárrell said. "All we have to do is show the protesters that we are changing the government, making some concessions to them. Then, I think we will be out of the woods."

Ybarra opened his mouth to offer an opinion, but Avalos raised his hand. "Let us hope," he said, "that Perón will slink away for good." Ybarra's hopes, rather than rising as his general suggested, wobbled and sank. Did these two old peacocks have no understanding of the uses of power? If they didn't, Ybarra was sure Perón did. He had seen the colonel's handsome, withdrawn face at army gatherings and recognized the mask of a deep thinker, planner, schemer. Ybarra was sure of it.

As they left the Casa Rosada, Avalos put a fatherly hand on Ybarra's shoulder. "Don't scowl so, Ramón," he said. "Have you talked to your brother? I asked him to speak to you."

It amazed Ybarra, this weak-kneed appeal, as if a big brother should be called in to subdue a petulant, overwrought child. His brother, a major in the quartermaster corps, had left him a message to call. But little brother was an adult now, not a six-year-old who was subject to the advice of a brother ten years his senior. Ramón held his tongue. Instead he lied and said he had spoken to him.

"He told you about the letters?"

Ybarra would be caught in the lie if he said yes, and in not obeying his superior officer if he said no. "Perón should be arrested," he said instead. "That's the only way we are going to have any chance of controlling what he does next."

"A girl was killed last night who looked like Evita Duarte," Avalos said. "I heard it from Justo Arietta, who has temporarily taken over the Federal Police."

"Has Velasco been pushed out?"

"Yes," Avalos said. "We need the police to back the army now. Velasco was loyal to Perón."

Ybarra was not sure Arietta had the cojones for the job. "What about this murder?"

Avalos shook his head. "The dead girl was a nobody, but the police think whoever murdered her was after the actress."

Ybarra thought for a second. "That would give us an excuse to incarcerate the actress, too," he said. "We can put the proud Evita into protective custody." He warmed to this idea. "If Perón and his hussy are both in jail, they will not be able to incite the rabble against the government, as I am convinced they will."

Avalos gave him a curious look. "You know I take your thoughts on this subject seriously, Ramón, but in this case, I think we have bigger fish to fry than the pipsqueak radio-novella actress. I have arranged for the officer corps to meet us at the Paz Palace. We are going there now. We have to reorganize ourselves for any eventuality. The faster we put together a new government, the safer we will be. There are too many dangers that could await us."

Their car took ten minutes to get through a small but determined group of pro-Perón demonstrators who had taken up a post blocking the thirty-foot arch that guarded the entrance to the Palacio Paz, the military headquarters of Buenos Aires. The massive mansion with its mansard roof and majestic facade was supposed to be a bastion of strength. Ybarra had his doubts.

Inside, three hundred military men heard their new secretary of war call for elections at the first possible moment. Lieutenant Ramón Ybarra, tortured by his scratchy, hot uniform, listened with rising anger while Argentina's top military men toyed with totally inadequate strategies. Nothing they considered doing would put Perón permanently out of the way, much less reestablish the army's dominance. Perón's supporters would rise up all over the country. The noisy group outside these very windows were not the only workers who would march. Pro-Perón demonstrations were already under way up north in Jujuy. Well, if they were not going to solve the problem, he had to try.

As the meeting broke up, Ybarra gave the high sign to his fellow lieutenant, Francisco Rocco. "Cisco," he said, smiling as if he were going to invite Rocco to a soccer match. When they were close enough not to be overheard, he said, "I have to be at Campo de Mayo tomorrow for an early conference. Meet me at ten thirty in the officer's mess for a coffee."

———

After leaving the *modista*'s shop, Roberto Leary spent the day digging for information to back up his theory that whoever had murdered Luz Garmendia had been after Eva Duarte. By noon, after hours without progress, he despaired of getting anywhere. The murderer had left no clues at the scene. All Leary could do was think about what the possible motive might be and work backward. Her father, her ex-lover Torres, of course, but everything in Buenos Aires seemed to be about politics these days. Even the death of a simple nobody like Luz Garmendia. That she could so easily be mistaken for Evita must have had something to do with the killer's going after her.

Leary focused on trying to find out the names of outspoken anti-Perónists who targeted their venom at Eva Duarte, people who might have thought that killing the actress would further weaken Juan Perón. Leary's was a weary endeavor. Millions wanted the now-former vice president and minister out of the way, but most people Leary spoke to scoffed at the idea that a woman could have any influence whatsoever on the power structure. They imagined that the wives of the mighty could have a bit of private clout, but they believed such women knew enough to keep themselves in the background or real men kept them there. As for mistresses, they were playthings. If a man didn't think enough of a woman to marry her, she would never be able to change the state of the nation. Leary wondered about this conventional wisdom.

Watching what happened in his own family had convinced him that a determined woman who had a man's ear could certainly sway him. All the more so if she also had access to the more vulnerable parts of his body.

Leary had to find out who might hate the actress enough to have done her harm. He thought around in circles until the light suddenly dawned on him. He punched himself in the forehead when he finally realized where to look. All the powerful of Buenos Aires had spies watching their assumed enemies, and Perón must have had a network of thousands of snoops.

Leary asked around in his office and found one of his fellow investigators who knew Colonel Domingo Mercante, Perón's greatest adherent, a fellow colonel who was known to act as Perón's chief of staff. Mercante would be the man who knew everything. If anyone could identify Eva Duarte's major detractors, he could.

Mercante seemed standoffish when Leary first called, but when Leary told him about Luz Garmendia's murder just following Perón's farewell rally at Perú and Alsina and that the girl was an Evita Duarte look-alike, Mercante immediately gave him a name: the rogue union leader Tulio Puglisi. "He gets vicious when he talks about her," Mercante said. "And despite his anti-Perón sentiments, he was there that afternoon."

Leary thanked Mercante, but he was sorry to suspect Puglisi. He had met the young union man while investigating a break-in at the National Shoe Makers Union office.

Puglisi was passionate about his work, something Leary envied because he used to feel that way, too. The last thing a demoralized detective needed was to investigate a man he liked for such a miserable crime.

It took the rest of the afternoon, going through files at the office of a friend who worked for the newspaper *Crítica*, to find a photo of Puglisi in the paper's morgue—where they kept all their backup information.

Leary took the clipping and chose to show it to the winsome tango dancer who had been with Luz Garmendia at the rally. He told himself she was his best witness and that it was information, not the girl, he was after. In any case, he knew where he could find her after dark.

Late that evening, Roberto Leary entered a bar on the ground floor of an elegant gray cement building that would have been built of stone if it had been in Paris. Here in the "Paris of the South," the architects had pretensions of elegance but only lowly materials with which to build.

When he entered the Club Gardel, the room, four steps down from the sidewalk, was almost as dark as the gloomy street outside. He did not pay the entrance fee; cops never did. He checked his hat and made his way through the knot of young men blocking the bar.

The band was playing "La Violetera," and the dance floor was packed with couples circling in tight formation. Without moving his body, he could feel how his muscles would respond to the music. It had been too long since he had danced, or known a woman he wanted to dance with. He was a cop now, on the trail of a possible witness to a bloody murder. Pilar was known to be here four, five nights a week. He was sure to find her on a Thursday, the night that regulars never missed, when the crowd was thick and excitement high, but when it was still possible to really dance, as it often was not in the crush of Friday and Saturday mob scenes.

Aware that his upper body had begun to sway to the music, he pushed his way through to the bar and ordered dry vermouth on the rocks. He took the drink and plowed back out through tight groups of working-class muchachos to watch the couples as they passed under the spotlight near the bandstand. Most of them were in close embrace, some wonderful dancers, obviously accustomed to dancing together. Light glinted off the metal edges of the bandoneón as the player extended and squeezed the instrument and made heartrending music.

Leary recognized the girl's hair first—straight, shining black, bobbed to jaw length and swinging like silk fringe as she turned her head from side to side with the movements of the dance. Her red dress hugged her ass, with a slit halfway up her leg, giving her room to step. She and her partner disappeared around to the other side of the crowded floor. Leary sipped his drink and waited for the song to end.

When Pilar spotted Leary coming toward her as the next number was about to begin, her heart beat with fear of being questioned about Luz's murder, but she could not resist him. She let go of Mariano's hand and moved toward the detective without a backward glance. She thought she saw in the intention in his eyes a *cabecco,* a look that was an invitation to dance. She held out her hand to him, as the strains of "Yira, Yira" began, happy for the musicians' choice. He took her hand, kissed it, and let it go. "Can I buy you a drink?"

Her heart sank. There were a few things she would like to do with this man. Dance, to begin with. But talk about Luz's murder was not one of them. "Thank you, yes."

They took their drinks to the corner nearest the door. A couple of the club regulars snuffed out their cigarettes in a black Bakelite ashtray, got up, and gave them the tiny table. They sat across from each other on bentwood chairs, and Leary put his head near hers to be heard over the music and the chat of the crowd filling the aisle between the hatcheck and the bar. "You dance beautifully," he said.

"I would gladly dance with you." Perhaps this night would live up to her hopes after all.

His dark eyes smiled, then turned serious. "I want to ask you about a man who was at the rally the afternoon before Luz was killed. I am wondering if you saw him, and if he might have followed her afterwards." He reached into the inside breast pocket of his jacket and took out a newspaper clipping and placed it on the table between them. He pointed to a man in suit, sitting at a desk with two other men. He was young and good-looking, with dark wavy hair and light eyes. He was smiling broadly in the photo. The caption identified the man as Tulio Puglisi, a director of the National Shoe Makers Union.

She shook her head. "He's young to have such an important position." The walls next to Leary and behind him were mirrored, so when she looked up she saw two of him and wondered if one was a cop and the other a dancer.

Leary asked again if she had seen that Puglisi fellow at the rally. "He is about my height," he said.

"No," she said and shook her head again. "I don't remember seeing him. There were a lot of people there." She hated to disappoint him, but it frightened her to her core to think the murderer might kill her because she was a potential witness. Her reflection in the mirror behind Leary's head frowned at her. She did her best to change that look to a smile.

He shoved the photo back into his pocket and drained his drink. The band took up "Arrabal Amargo." "I'll have that dance now," he said, with just the right combination of request and command.

He took her hand and led her to the dance floor. Despite the press of the crowd, he held her in open embrace. He was just a bit taller than she in her high heels. He held his cheek against her forehead, but their bodies apart. The narrow space of air between them seemed infused with the pulsating rhythm and the nostalgia of the music, but though he led her with the intensity of longing in the song, he never closed the embrace. Only their ankles and knees brushed as their legs passed each other's. His cheek was smooth, recently shaved, and carried the minty smell of shaving soap.

He never let go of her hand, not even when the band took a break and he took her to the bar for a drink. They danced every dance. He spoke hardly a word. As the crowd thinned and gave them room, his improvisations of steps and pauses, the passion with which he danced made her wild for him. Just before dawn, the band signaled the end by playing "Adios Muchachos," the song to which no one danced because it was the last song the great Carlos Gardel had sung before he boarded a plane that crashed and ended his life. The dozen or so couples still left on the dance floor stood swaying almost imperceptibly, watching the bandoneón open and close, the fingers of the guitar player on the strings, listening to Mariano sing the words.

Leary drove her home and kissed her chastely on the cheek and then drove his wonderful red American car away, the headlights illuminating the buildings as he rounded the curve at the end of the cobblestoned street and disappeared, leaving her alone with her desire.

At midnight, the president of the nation took to the airwaves, announcing that elections would be held at the earliest possible moment. In hastily arranged meetings, half the army brass still hoped to maintain Fárrell in office. The other half supported a solution put forward by professors and students, that the Supreme Court take power in the interim. The other armed services saw this as impossible. The navy reminded anyone who would listen that the court had no power. Who on that court knew how to run a country? No one.

Many wondered whether anyone could rule this nation, divided as it was.

FRIDAY, OCTOBER 12

The next morning, while the newspapers carried no truthful news and a whirlwind of rumors terrified the citizenry, Hernán Mantell gave Claudia a good-bye kiss. She had kept him up until the wee hours, protesting, "It's my fault. I thought I was helping her by bringing her out of the misery she lived in, but I brought her to her death." She wept at intervals and talked about how the death on her doorstep would affect her business. Then went back to guilt, this time over thinking about money when Luz Garmendia lay on a slab in the morgue.

Hernán felt guilty, too, for wanting any excuse to escape her tears. When his editor called just as dawn was breaking to ask him to cover the latest political insanities, he took the urgency of his assignment as an alibi to get away. The president had called for the resignation of all of his cabinet except Avalos. The street in front of the Paz Palace, where the military club was housed, was filling up with students shouting antimilitary slogans and calling for the arrest of Perón and the return to a constitutional government. "I am covering the unions today," he told Claudia. "It looks as if they might call a general strike. If they do, what's left of the government will go over the cliff. God knows what will happen after that."

Claudia blew her nose and touched his shoulder as he went out. "Be careful, *querido*," she called after him. She knew how glad he must be to escape her whining. She tried to be angry with him for leaving her, but it was too obvious, even to her in her grief, that she had become totally frozen with self-pity. She needed to do something to expiate her guilt.

After he left, she felt compelled to run away from her pain. She dressed and went out to see if Lázaro Torres had come to work and to see how he would react to the news of Luz's death. She convinced herself that she would be able to see the guilt in his face. Nothing could take away her own culpability, but she had to do something to bring the animal who had murdered Luz to justice. The detective, Roberto Leary, was eager enough considering that he was a Buenos Aires policeman, but he remained unconvinced that Torres was his man. He was sticking to his far-fetched notion that whoever had stabbed Luz thought he was killing Evita. If he was right, Claudia could spend the rest of her life overwhelmed with loss.

She was the catalyst for Luz's delusions about Evita. She

worried that her own insistence on Torres as the assailant was just an attempt to rationalize away her own part in the murder. But there were plenty of reasons to suspect the gardener, regardless of what Leary said. Torres was a man abandoned by a woman. Nice men like Leary always found it hard to accept what Claudia understood very well—that when men killed women it was usually for egotistical reasons. She had heard too many stories of abuse gone overboard, of women's lives taken to avenge masculine honor. It was part of the air Argentine men breathed to imagine they had a right to sacrifice any female they thought had betrayed them. If it wasn't Torres who had taken Luz's sad young life, it was certainly the girl's father. Hadn't Garmendia said as much to Pilar's face in that club where she danced?

Claudia called Pilar and told her to stay home. There would be no fancy dresses to sew today. Then she went out into bright sunshine that hurt her eyes after all the dull days of the past week. But there was no Lázaro in the garden. She searched out Raul Llorca, the manager of the building, and learned that Torres had not shown up for work—not today, and not yesterday, either. Another indication that he was the culprit.

"He goes on the drunk," Llorca said. "If he weren't the best gardener I've ever known, I would have gotten rid of him years ago." Raul, by contrast, was the worst building manager Claudia could imagine. In the eight years she had lived here, she had never seen him do a lick of actual work, unless one considered it work to stand around watching other people shovel gravel or polish floors.

Claudia bought some eggs and vegetables from the purveyor who came around with his horse and cart. She delivered them to her father for his lunch and left again. This time to pay a condolence call on Miguel Garmendia—a visit she hoped would ease her guilt and maybe tell her something she could pass on to Roberto Leary.

At that same midmorning hour, the beautiful blue sky of what had promised to be a perfect spring day clouded over. Lieutenant Ramón Ybarra, walking across the leafy grounds of the Campo de Mayo forty-five kilometers north of Buenos Aires, approved of the change in weather. With thousands marching in the streets and violence breaking out in the city center at regular intervals, gray skies were more fitting for the mood of the nation. No one in Argentina was happy, least of all Ybarra, who pulled off his gloves, removed his cap, and placed it under his arm as he entered under the white arched doorway of the officer's mess. He set his facial expression to neutral.

In the cool of the high-ceilinged interior, he loosened the wide belt around his waist a notch and unbuttoned the top button of his jacket. How long would it be, he wondered, before the order for summer uniforms would come through? The heavy, dark wool was beginning to tell on his nerves.

Older officers said one got accustomed to the scratchy cloth and stifling weight of the uniform, but he doubted he ever would.

Ybarra was accepting an espresso in a delicate china cup from the hands of a server behind a linen-draped table, when Francisco Rocco, his fellow lieutenant and closest friend, entered the stately room. The gangly Cisco was an ally worth having. He had, more than other officers of Ramón's generation, reason to join the fight against Perón and the do-nothing policies of the Fárrell–Avalos regime. Just last week, Rocco had endured a dreadful slap in the face thanks to the colonel and his whore of an actress. Ybarra's Basque temper flared just thinking about it, especially since Eva Duarte was from Basques, too. The blood of the conquistadores flowed in her veins as well as his, but she was a blot on them all—bastard child and *puta* that she was.

Rocco had expected to be appointed the next secretary of communications. President Fárrell had promised him the post. But Perón had given it instead to one of his flunkies, Oscar Nicolini, a grunt of a civil servant, and worst of all one who had endeared himself to Eva Duarte.

Ybarra greeted his friend, took another coffee, and handed it to him. He led Cisco to a table in a quiet corner. With his back to the room, he began the spiel he had been rehearsing through most of a largely sleepless night. "My friend," he said, "the government is on the brink of collapse. Yet, President Fárrell and General Avalos are doing nothing. It is time for stronger and braver men to take charge of Argentina's future."

Francisco Rocco sat back in his chair. Astonishment and then fear burned in his eyes. "What are you saying, Ramón? You can't mean what I think you said."

Ybarra leaned forward. "Just listen to me before you reject what I am saying. Argentina is at a crossroads. I am with Fárrell and Avalos all the time. They are totally unprepared to handle the situation. In fact, they deny that the nation is in danger. Someone has to save it. Since they will not, I say we have to."

"But . . . but . . ."

Ybarra gripped Rocco's upper arm. "Not buts. We can, and we must."

Francisco sat up straight. "But how?"

Ybarra hiked his chair closer and looked over his shoulder. There were two young officers-in-training across the massive room near the fireplace. A couple of waiters busy setting tables for lunch were the only other men left in the room. "You are in touch with a lot of the line officers here, Cisco. We have to act with dispatch. While I am here, I am going to talk to Novara. I am sure he will see things our way. He was outraged about the Nicolini appointment."

"He is outraged about a lot of things."

"You see?"

"Are you sure Joaquín will join in? He is a major."

"Yes. I have already had some tentative words with him, but I could not go into detail over the telephone. You should have heard him last night. I could hear the foam in his mouth over the phone lines. You need to talk to Cieza and

Garín. They are captains and command tanks and artillery. I am sure we can get them to agree, too. They have both complained bitterly to me in the last two weeks."

"A mutiny?"

"A putsch. It may not even come to that. If we get the right men with troops and weapons behind us, we may very well get Avalos to cave in and give the order he should have already issued."

"What about your brother? He's a major, too."

"Forget about my brother."

Fear flickered again in Rocco's eyes.

"What is it, Cisco? You do think the army needs to crack down on the chaos, don't you?"

Rocco nodded but not entirely convincingly. "My problem is that I can't get over being thrown aside in favor of Nicolini."

"Right," Ybarra said. "And look at what's going on. Perón was pushed out almost a week ago. Has Fárrell or Avalos reversed Nicolini's shameful appointment? Have they given you what should have been rightfully yours?"

"No," Rocco said vehemently. "My wife is pregnant with our second kid. She was already looking for a larger apartment when we got the word that I was out and Nicolini was in. She cried about having to live in such a small place with two children."

"So? Are you with us? Are you going to help us force those fools to give you what should have rightfully been yours?"

Francisco Rocco straightened his back and squared his shoulders like a man at attention. "Yes," he said. "Yes, I will."

Ybarra outlined his plan: which troops would go on standby, which officers must be kept out of the plot.

Rocco drank it all in. "It could work," he said.

"It worked for the men who did it in 1943. It will work for us now." Ybarra rose and looked at his watch. "I have to go meet Novara. Call me at home tonight and let me know what happens with the other two. Cieza will be called 'the Roman,' Garín, 'the tailor.' Just call me and tell me if the Roman and the tailor have bought tickets to the game."

Rocco stood up and for a second Ybarra was afraid he was going to salute. They shook hands, and Ybarra marched out to meet Joaquín Novara near the statue of Manuel Belgrano halfway between the enlisted men's barracks and the entrance to the post.

By eleven that morning, Hernán Mantell was making the rounds of the union halls, looking for information on whether the workers had any plans to call a general strike and whether they thought they could restore Perón to power by doing so. In the dim offices of the leather workers, Mantell sought out Tulio Puglisi, a man with a mind prone to see beyond the obvious. Tulio greeted him with news that had just come over the radio: a group of students had stormed the Paz Palace and were demanding that the Supreme Court take over interim rule of the country and hold elections at the first possible moment. They wanted their enemy Perón in jail.

"It kills me," Puglisi said, talking and exhaling cigarette smoke at the same time. "Every bone in my body despises those privileged sons of the upper classes, but I find I have more in common with the students than I do with my brothers in the union movement when it comes to my opinion of Perón."

"Your guys want to strike for the colonel, then?" Hernán asked.

Puglisi took one last drag and crushed out his cigarette in the overflowing glass ashtray on his desk. "Not quite as bad as that. They are talking about a strike, but they are holding off on the question of whether they should announce that it is in support of Perón."

"What do you think will happen, Tulio?"

"It's Hobson's choice. If the skilled-workers' unions decide to throw their weight behind Perón, we will find ourselves in his pockets. I've finally gotten them to consider what a mistake that would be. But if the generals get their way, we will very likely lose the gains we've gotten from the bastard. If you ask me, we will—"

The telephone rang. Puglisi grabbed it. He listened, grunting intermittently, combing his fingers through his dark, unruly hair. After a long pause, he said, "Yes." And then, "If it works out that way, okay." He dropped the black receiver into its cradle with a heavy clunk and turned to Hernán. "That was a source of mine. A janitor in the Casa Rosada.

Fárrell has decided to issue an arrest warrant for Perón. The justices are doing the paperwork."

Hernán wondered at the way spy networks worked so efficiently in Buenos Aires when nothing else seemed to. "What do you think this means for the unions?"

"I just told you. If we don't fight back, our pensions, our shorter hours, our safe-work rules could all go down the toilet."

Hernán took out his notebook to get the quote. "It's obvious then. You'll strike." It was only half a question.

"I think you can count on the unions doing something," Puglisi replied. "But I'm going to fight tooth and nail for us to hold on to our progress despite Perón's downfall. If we decide to defend our gains by supporting him, we'll wind up with that fascist not only back in power but single-handedly so."

"How, if he's in jail?"

Puglisi looked stunned by Hernán's naïveté. "If you ask me, throwing the bastard in jail might incite the low-level guys out on the periphery to rise up. There are hundreds of thousands of them, and they don't understand subtleties. They see only one choice. They have been trained by Perón to worship Perón."

Hernán wrote down the sentence—a perfect quote, if he ever got to write about this. A big *if.* He put his pencil behind his ear. "Can the unskilled men get it together without leadership? Who whips up the *descamisados* if Perón is in jail?"

"The actress, for one."

"The actress?"

"Can you think of anyone better to stir up the masses? She has that intensity, that little tremble in her voice that makes the commoners believe her. Did you hear that shameless program she did on the radio, praising Perón on his principles? Nothing to entertain. Just glorifying her boyfriend. And people listened to it because that voice of hers beguiled them."

"Surely it is more complicated than that."

"Not in my book. This is all about Perón. He blames the foreigners, reactionaries, the upper classes for all of Argentina's problems, and his supporters cheer him in the streets for saying so. But when he criticizes self-centered politicians, he is really describing himself. For me, he is a prime egotist. Everything he does is aimed at increasing his own power."

"Come on, Tulio. You talk about the *descamisados* not being capable of subtle thinking, yet you are acting like a sledgehammer yourself."

A man in a gray suit and a brown fedora had come in and was standing nearby. He looked as if he was waiting to talk to Tulio, who didn't seem to notice but just went on ranting. "I am not saying Perón hasn't lifted the lives of the lowest-level guys in the slaughterhouses. But if any union resists his so-called leadership, he gets a rival union started that will be loyal to him and puts the recalcitrant group out of business. And sends its leaders out to the prison camps on the Pampas. My family in Sicily had enough of that sort of thing with Mussolini—a man, by the way, that Perón admired greatly.

Perón has this friend Freude. He goes to Freude's house to meet with Nazis. I am telling you he's a Nazi; he's so like Hitler he even has a girlfriend named Eva." They all laughed at that: Hernán, the man in the gray suit; even Tulio saw how over the top he had gotten. He held up his hands to stop the guffaws. "It's the truth, though. If he gets a free hand, it will be the end of freedom in this country."

The brown fedora moved closer, and the stranger chimed right in, without an introduction or even a greeting, "What about the actress? Do you think she will have a role in this?"

This guy wasn't any reporter Hernán had ever met.

Puglisi looked at him. "What the fuck are you doing here, Leary?"

The man took off his hat and held out his hand to Hernán. "Detective Roberto Leary," he said. Mantell shook his hand and wondered if this cop was here to arrest the union leaders. If the army was going to crack down, they might very well start with cracking heads in the union halls.

Leary put that fear immediately to rest. "I was interested in what you were saying about Eva Duarte and the role she might have in bringing back Perón."

Puglisi's blue eyes lit up. "Are you going to arrest her, I hope?"

"I'm not sure on what grounds I would do such a thing."

Tulio grinned. "It's too bad hypocrisy isn't against the law. She talks on the radio about Perón and identifies with the poor as if she is still one of them, but she is one of the richest working women in Buenos Aires now. Look at her jewels, her expensive clothes. We are on the brink of civil war here and she cares more about how she looks than whether her country will bleed to death."

Hernán chuckled at Puglisi's ardor and said nothing about his lady friend making those expensive dresses "If hypocrisy were against the law, Tulio, Roberto here would be able fill up the jails in half a day with clerics and philanthropists."

"To say nothing of every politician who ever lived," Tulio said, "starting with Pontius Pilate." The twinkle in Puglisi's eyes was going full strength now.

The policeman's expression turned serious. "Does the Duarte woman's possible role scare you as much as you were saying when I came in?" he asked.

Hernán could not resist an opinion. "If she does take a role, it will be clumsy and harsh. If she wants to help her colonel, she should keep out of the limelight."

The cop gave his head an almost imperceptible shake and concentrated on Puglisi. "I am interested in what you think, Tulio."

The union leader's smile vanished. "She is a powerful personality," was all Puglisi said.

Claudia had heard from Luz that her father and her grandmother lived in the part of town where Claudia's own father had grown up. But during the heavy immigration at the end of the last century, when newcomers packed in twelve to a room, the rents had doubled. Little Gregorio and his mother, a Paraguayan war widow and schoolteacher, had been pressed out by the high prices. Now the neighborhood was considered quite unsavory. Claudia looked at her watch. She wouldn't want to be caught there after dark, but at this time of year the sun didn't go down till seven. She still had plenty of daylight to get there and pay her respects before darkness fell. She didn't care about Luz's father, but the girl had had a grandmother who must have loved her. Claudia could find out from her where and when Luz's funeral would be. She bought a bouquet of white peonies at the flower stall next to the Art Nouveau Subte entrance.

The train was nearly empty. People were keeping to home. But when Claudia emerged onto the streets of the working-class neighborhood, shoppers were out and about, mostly buying food for their suppers. The area around the subway stop was busy with open-air vendors, the sidewalks cluttered with racks of cheap clothing and tubs of seafood on ice outside a fishmonger's store.

Claudia asked directions from a stooped granny pushing an old wicker baby carriage and picked her way down a narrow, gloomy street to a small plaza in front of an ancient church in ill repair. The barrio might have been quaintly attractive were it not for the squalor.

At the corner of the Calle Martínez, Garmendia's street, a grocery displayed crates of pathetic little oranges stacked on rusty racks. Watermelons rested right on the cement pavement. Prices were scrawled in white chalk on a scrap of plywood painted black and resting against the storefront. Two tomatoes rotted in a greasy puddle in the gutter. Claudia's heart sank, imagining young Luz buying food in this sort of putrid place to make the lunches Torres so disdained.

Number 39 was a dilapidated, once-elegant town house whose window boxes now contained only dead weeds. The dark door at street level was not brown, not black, not green—some ugly color between them all. The tiny vestibule smelled of cat urine and neglect. A sign taped to the doorbell said, OUT OF ORDER, KNOCK HARD. A small dog yapped somewhere inside. A list of tenants indicated that Luz's family lived on the fourth floor.

Claudia hesitated to go in, but she had come this far. Tears welled in her eyes for the lost girl who had run away from this sad home. And to go where? To Torres, who undoubtedly lived in another such miserable hovel, which the desperate Luz thought would be a safe haven of happiness. A sob escaped Claudia.

Some children pushed into the entryway behind her, opened the inner door without a key, and ran up the stairs. Claudia entered behind them and started up after them. The hallway was dim, lit only by a single bare bulb on each floor. The voice of Alberto Acuña singing a tango on a radio spilled from the open door of a ground-floor flat. More schoolchildren in their white smocks, coming home for lunch, plowed in from the street and ran ahead of her as she walked up dusty, broken marble steps to the door of the fourth-floor apartment that Miguel Garmendia shared with his mother. She was a bit breathless when she knocked.

A slovenly old woman opened the door.

Luz's grandmother frowned when Claudia told her her name and offered her condolences and the flowers, but the old lady let the door swing open and stood back to let the visitor enter. The room was shabby and sparsely furnished. It smelled of stewing beef.

The grandmother took the bouquet Claudia offered and put it on a battered oak chair. Claudia doubted there was anything resembling a vase in this place. "How did you know Luz?" the old woman asked.

Unprepared for the question, Claudia blurted out the first thing that came into her mind: "I met her at the market. I heard about the murder from a friend of mine who works at a shoe store on Florida."

A large man sitting at a table against the far wall with a whiskey bottle and a glass in front of him growled at her statement. He couldn't be anyone but Luz's father. "Oh," he said, "then you know the bitch who owns the dress shop."

Claudia took one hesitant step over the threshold. "Do you know her?" she asked.

"Do I look like I order my clothes from a fancy *modista*? Does she?" He jerked his thumb toward his mother.

"I am so sorry for your loss, Señor Garmendia," Claudia said. She kept her place near the open door. "You knew where she worked then? Luz didn't think you did."

The man stood up and swayed. "I asked a few questions at a tango club. A guy I knew saw Luz there with some little whore. What is all this to you?" He brandished a fist, but did not move toward her. He started to weep.

Claudia held her place. Though still wary of the man, a part of her heart wanted to believe his tears. He had, after all, lost his only child. But something told her any movement on her part could bring on violence.

In a few seconds he proved her instincts right. He sniveled and wiped his nose on his sleeve and started to shout. "You can't fool me. You must be the bitch who gave her the job. I can tell by your fancy clothes. I ought to beat you within an inch of your life. That little bitch dishonored me, and you helped her do it. You deserve to die, too." He took a step forward.

Claudia backed out the door and slammed it behind her. Praying he was too drunk to make it down the stairs without falling, she sped down as fast as her platform heels would allow.

The door behind her opened. "That's right. Run away. But I know where to find you if I want to," Garmendia shouted after her as she turned on the last landing. She made it to the front door and ran from the building.

Claudia's heart did not stop thudding until she was back on the Subte, on her way back to her shop. In Buenos Aires, the very size of the city had always seemed to offer anonymity. The *porteños* all lived with the assumption that the complexity of their city protected them. That if they wanted to, they could hide in plain sight among the millions of other people and be safe. Claudia had assumed, for instance, that Torres would not discover where Luz worked, even though he worked at the building where Claudia lived. Yet, Garmendia, who had no connection whatsoever with anyone in Luz's new life, had found her by coincidence because someone he knew had accidentally seen Luz at the Gardel with Pilar. Evidently, that someone had also told Garmendia where Pilar worked.

If Garmendia had managed to find Luz, it would have been even easier for Torres. If he so much as suspected that Claudia had anything to do with Luz's escape from his grip, Torres would have been able to find the girl at Claudia's shop in an hour. And if he knew about it now? He could come to her apartment door anytime.

She looked out the window of the Subte car; the darkness of the tunnel reflected back only her own mournful expression. In a city this size the girl should have been able to disappear from those dreadful people. Having discovered where Luz worked, had Garmendia then waited outside the shop for his daughter and killed her? He had wept over her death. Could he have faked those tears? She didn't believe he could be such a clever actor. Perhaps he had butchered his daughter in one of his drunken rages and later repented it. Or perhaps Pilar was right, that Torres had killed Luz. It would have been even easier for him. Especially if the brute suspected Luz's connection to Claudia. Even if he didn't, Luz had told Pilar she had seen him at the rally. He could easily have followed them to the shop and then lain in wait until poor little Luz was alone.

Claudia shook her head and her reflection in the window shook its head back. She needed a coffee and a cigarette. Then she would try to talk to Roberto Leary. She had to persuade him to give up his harebrained theory about the murderer wanting to kill Eva Duarte. Either Luz's father or Torres had robbed the girl's life just when it was happiest. Whoever it had been must be made to pay.

That afternoon, Ramón Ybarra escorted a group of citizens into General Avalos's new office in the Casa Rosada. When the general took over as minister of war, he had eschewed occupying the desk that Perón had so recently abandoned. He took instead a smaller place, closer to President Fárrell.

By their English suits and expensive shoes, the men of this delegation would likely take a position Ybarra could support. These were people he might find useful if he and Rocco could get enough officers on their side to make his planned uprising work.

Ybarra carefully introduced himself to each one and made sure they would remember the charming lieutenant when the right time came. He showed them into Avalos's office. The obvious leader of the group took Avalos's outstretched hand.

"General," he said, all cordiality. "Thank you for receiving us. I can only imagine how many things you have to attend to today. My name is Osvaldo Strade."

"Yes, I recognize you from the pictures in *Crítica*." Avalos indicated the chairs opposite his desk and invited them to sit, but there were five of them and only two seats.

"No, no," Strade said, holding up a hand. "We will speak our piece quickly and let you get on with your important work. We just want to make sure you understand how serious our objections are to Colonel Perón's policies. Especially, we feel that the impossibly generous concessions he doled out in that impudent broadcast Wednesday must be rescinded at once."

Ybarra knew better. If he had his way, no such step would be taken until the might of the army had taken firm control over the populace. He wondered that these obviously wealthy and powerful men did not see the inadvisability, even stupidity of negating Perón's latest pronouncement before a true military state was established. Until then, all the workers in the packinghouses would need to hear was that the lily-livered government was stripping them of their gains. The riffraff would be up in arms in hours. They would not even need that whore of an actress to stir them up. These men would have their way, but not until after he and his friends cracked down on the monkey populations in the unions.

Ybarra managed to keep a straight face while Avalos gently broke the news to Strade and his followers that their request could not be granted. Then the general told them something that he had not yet revealed to Ybarra: "I can tell you in the strictest confidence that Colonel Perón will be taken into custody very soon. But I tell you without reservation that if any word of this leaks out before the fact, the arrest will not take place. The order is in the hands of the justices, but the law must be followed to the letter. I take it I have your word, as gentlemen, that you will not breathe a hint of this outside this room."

Two days ago, Ybarra would have rejoiced at this news, which brought broad smiles to the faces of their visitors. Today, however, Ybarra was not sure how he felt. If the plan he was hatching was to come to fruition, Rocco and the other junior officers needed to see themselves as Argentina's only hope. Any decisive move by Fárrell and Avalos against Perón would dilute their resolve.

Each visitor gave a signal of his oath not to tell: blessing himself or making a cross over his lips and his heart like a schoolboy in short pants. One even put his left hand on an imaginary Bible while he raised his right and said, "You have my word."

Osvaldo Strade spoke again. "It would be best if we could tell the students outside the Palacio Paz what is going to happen. They are counting on us to convince you. I am afraid they will be outraged if we are forced to report that we failed to get action against the colonel."

"I am sorry," Avalos answered. "That would be out of the question. There would be no way to control the information if you shared it so broadly. A leak at this point would jeopardize the entire matter."

The smiles left the faces of the delegates. They filed out in silence. Ybarra escorted them down the hall, eager now to get rid of them so he could find a private spot where he could telephone Cisco and tell him this latest news. When their party reached the stairs to the exit, his secretary approached him and put a pink telephone message in his hand. It was from his brother, who insisted on seeing him before the day was out. He crumbled it and stuffed it into his jacket pocket as he accompanied Strade and his coterie of magnates down the regal marble staircase to the front door and saw them off. As quickly as he could, he found an empty office at the rear of the third floor and dialed Francisco Rocco's number out at Campo de Mayo. He was able to convince Cisco that they still needed to be ready—just in case.

"But we will not move unless we have to." Cisco's voice was tentative, almost fearful.

"Of course not."

Before the end of the day, the captains of industry were proved more prescient about the situation than the generals of the army. That evening, Ybarra got more grist for his mill. Enraged students stormed through the great archway at the entrance to military headquarters at Palacio Paz and attacked the building. At 9:00 P.M., a shoot-out erupted between the students and the police. One man was killed and more than fifty others were wounded, including a Jewish-Italian immigrant woman who had done nothing more radical than take a walk in her own neighborhood with her husband, her daughter, and her young son.

In the face of this further chaos, late on that moonless night, President Fárrell finally signed a duly prepared arrest warrant for Perón. In his apartment in the Recoleta district, Ybarra had fallen asleep over a map where he had been planning attack routes between the Campo de Mayo and the center of the city. The telephone awakened him well before dawn. Avalos deputized him to go to Perón's apartment with a squadron of soldiers to make the arrest.

As Ybarra suspected, Perón had already gone into hiding. Over the shouted objections of Perón's chauffeur, Domingo Mercante told Ybarra where the colonel could be found. Mercante said that Perón had instructed him to reveal his whereabouts.

In his car, on his way back to his office to report that Perón was still at large, Ybarra passed a drunk in the street, shouting, "Viva Perón. Viva Perón." Ybarra spit out the window in the man's direction.

SATURDAY, OCTOBER 13

Though it was still dark, Juan Perón and Eva Duarte were awake and waiting in the house in Tres Bocas when the boat coming to arrest Perón approached. Jorge Webber and Domingo Mercante had beaten the arresting officers to the secluded retreat, Jorge hoping he could help Perón escape, and Mercante wanting only to prepare his friends for the inevitable and to see what help he could be at the last minute.

Perón immediately refused Jorge's pleas that he and Evita run away. The whole idea of fleeing like some worthless out-law depressed him even more than the thought of jail. "Please, Jorge, if you don't mind," he said, "go into the bathroom and pack up my razor and shaving soap. Get my cigarettes, and a few clean shirts and underclothes. I don't imagine they will deny me a few necessities while I am in custody."

Webber saluted, though he was not a soldier. He left the door to the bedroom open so he could hear the conversation in front of the fireplace as he quietly packed a bag for his colonel.

Mercante and Perón immediately turned their attention to how the situation could be rescued. As Webber expected, Evita insisted that they focus on the needs of the lowest workers. "The poor *grasitos*," she said. "Their hearts will be broken when they find out. Domingo, you must help them. If you can get them to rise up, they will save their hero. They would die for you, Juan. I know they would."

Perón put his arm around her shoulder. All the energy of the champion athlete that usually infused his body was drained. "You see, Domingo, why I chose her to be my other self? Her heart goes right to the *descamisados*. And no one I have ever met works as hard as she does. I thought I was a man who knew how to work hard. But she makes me feel like a lazy lout."

"What good will it do me without you?"

Mercante went to the front windows to look for the boat they all knew was coming. He glanced back at Evita and then at the colonel. "What do you think we should do next?" he asked Perón.

Perón turned away from her and gave Mercante a knowing look. "I am not sure we can come out of this on top," he said. "I will need a lot of help if I am going to stand up to my enemies. We will have to chart the best course through roiled waters. It will not be easy to find."

Evita began to pace. "Just tell me what you want me to do. I will be a fanatic for your cause."

Perón answered her, but he looked at Mercante when he did. "Your time has not yet come. You will know when to act, *mi gioviota*. In the meantime, I want you to stay safe and stand by me."

She studied him with that look of hers, of intense observation. She was where he wanted her: too off-kilter to rush about and make trouble. His future hung in the balance. But it was not just a tug-of-war between opposing factions in Argentina. More important to him were the forces within this tiny sylph of a woman—her swings between rage against injustice and hunger for fame. She was not enough of an actress to play her role well if he defined it for her. If he directed her too strongly, she would overdo her part. If he tried too hard to tone her down, he would freeze her into doing nothing. He had to step her along slowly until the time was right. Then she would do what he needed with all her heart, and her sincerity would be irresistible.

He turned to Mercante. "Domingo, will you look after her for me?" He caught Mercante's glance and saw that he understood the full import of what looking after Evita could mean.

"Certainly," Mercante said. He went to the window again. "No sign of it yet." He went back to Evita and took her hand. "Do you have anyplace where you can stay besides your apartment on Posadas? Demonstrators will focus on it. It will not be comfortable for you there."

"If there was a phone here, I would call Pierina Dealessi, a friend from my stage-acting days. She has always helped me when I needed her. As soon as we get back to Buenos Aires, I will ask her if I can stay with her. I know she will say yes." Pierina had taken Evita in many times when she was unknown and starving, in those dreary days before she had regular work.

They heard a boat approaching. At this hour in the off-season, it could only be the one they expected. Its engine roared like some huge and angry jaguar coming up the channel to hunt them. She went to Juan and embraced him, finding it impossible to hold back her tears or her outrage. "The generals have all the power at this moment. They have all the money and the guns, but we have heart. Heart will always win, because heart will never give up."

Jorge Webber closed the bag he was packing and carried it to the front door just as the knock came.

Evita embraced her colonel again. "They cannot defeat us. All you have to do is decide," she said with more passion than she had ever put into a mere performance on the radio.

Perón shook hands with Mercante. "This is not necessarily a bad thing, Domingo, to be out of the thick of the fray and to be seen as coming from outside."

Mercante grasped his friend's shoulder and nodded, but his face was grave, as if he wanted to but could not quite believe they could win.

When Evita walked out with Perón to the dock, she was shocked to see an enormous gunboat. ARA INDEPENDEN-

CIA, it said in white on its black bow. Did they think they needed such a monstrosity to take one compliant man to prison? A crew of seven stood at the ready on the deck. Obviously, those vipers in the military knew as well as she how strong Perón still was. Otherwise, they would have sent a little police launch, not this warship.

Perón was not so impressed. "Oh," he said, "my opponents have sent a ship of their own vintage—from the last century and ripe to go out of service."

In the pale light of the setting moon and the bright pools created by flashlights in the hands of the crew, Evita watched Perón board. He stood under an awning on the deck where he could see her waving from the dock. Though he affected his usual military carriage, she detected a tension in the way he held his head. Her fearless warrior was fighting hard for calm.

She stayed on, gazing at him until his beautiful smile disappeared into the predawn gloom.

When the great boat had departed, Evita, Mercante, and Jorge Webber returned to the house, and Webber closed the door against the chilly night. Mercante touched Evita's shoulder so tenderly that she thought he was going to tell her Perón was being taken away to be shot. "What is it?" she demanded.

"Yesterday I spoke to a detective of the Buenos Aires police force," Mercante said. "A girl was murdered this past Wednesday. Her name was Luz. She worked for your dressmaker."

Evita screamed so loud that Webber feared they would hear her on the departing gunboat. She wrung her hands until they turned red, threw herself into a chair, and beat her fists on the thick upholstery of its arms. "What? Why? Who could have done such a thing to the poor, powerless child?"

Webber grabbed Mercante by the elbow. "Are you crazy, telling her such news at a moment like this?" He wanted to hit Mercante, who was not only taller but infinitely more powerful in station.

Mercante peeled Webber's fingers off his arm. "You are forgetting yourself," he said, with the look of a man who has been pooped on by a pigeon. He went and knelt in front of the chair where Evita continued to bang her fists and weep. "Listen to me, Evita," he said. "The police think the girl could have been murdered because she was mistaken for you."

She looked at him with those intense dark eyes, now fearful behind the tears. "Why would anyone want to kill an actress?" she asked, but he could see that she already knew the answer.

He fingered his lapel pin, the flag of Argentina. "We must leave right away. I'll tell our boatman. I am going to take you back to the Calle Posadas. At the first possible moment, though, you must call your actress friend and arrange to go to her. You have to stay in a place where a possible assailant can't find you."

Aboard the *ARA Independencia,* Peron's captors took him to a military prison on the island of Martín Garcia, in the middle of the broad, brown Rio La Plata. When they asked Perón why he flashed his famous smile on seeing that damp and forbidding place, he said, "The irony of being taken to jail on a boat called *Independence* is not wasted on me." But that was not the only reason. It also occurred to him that use could be made of their choice of a prison, given that the man being jailed had just turned fifty, an age when a man was considered to be losing his strength. His captors had left themselves open to a creditable claim that he was too infirm to withstand hardship conditions.

Perón considered various ways in which he might escape his jail, and Evita, once she had settled in her temporary home with her friend Pierina Dealessi, focused her enormous energy on the same question. Taking advice from Domingo Mercante and Oscar Nicolini, she made an appointment with Attilio Bramuglia, a labor lawyer and Perón supporter.

Jorge Webber drove her to the attorney's office in the Packard, but the chauffeur warned her that the government would very likely take away the car, since it was not Perón's but went with a station he no longer occupied. Strangely, this detail, like the death of that poor young *modista*'s assistant, more than any of the momentous events of the past week, overwhelmed her and brought her to tears. Far worse things were happening in her life; they made her angry, but they had not made her weep. Her father had had a wonderful car, and she had lost that one when he left her family and went back to his real wife and legitimate children. Right now, she longed to have Perón back just as she had longed to have her papa back all those years ago out on the dusty, unforgiving plains of the Pampas. No one, no one was allowed to know this. She was glad no one but the chauffeur saw her fall apart at the very idea of losing the Packard.

She looked out the car window as they passed the palatial buildings of the capital city—the land of her childhood dreams. She thought of Luz, killed when she was less than a year older than Evita had been when she arrived here. That child had died before she had even dreamed a dream of her own.

Another strange thought fell into her head, like something out of a radio novella—that the murderer had killed the girl not because he mistook her for Evita but to warn Evita that her life was on the line if she did not stand down in her support of Perón. If she did what so many of his supporters had been urging her to do, to stir up the *descamisados*, she could be the next to die.

She did not even know if Perón knew that the girl Luz had existed. She could not remember mentioning her, a nonentity, to him. Why had Mercante told her the news as soon as Perón was taken away? He had seemed to be warning her to be careful. She wanted to trust Mercante as much as Perón did. But how could she be sure of him, or anyone? The wisest man she knew was locked away from her. Her heart twisted with the loneliness of not being able to seek her colonel's advice, of being robbed of his protection.

Roberto Leary went to work that morning with more energy than he had brought with him in years, intent on pursuing the murder case even though no one besides himself and Luz Garmendia's friends cared about the girl's death. Everything Leary had heard from Puglisi's own mouth made Tulio a prime suspect. But Mercante had given up Puglisi's name too readily. And he had mentioned no one else. Why? There must be others who despised the actress, might have meant her harm. Leary decided to go back to Mercante—this time in person. He wanted to look the man in the eyes.

They met for coffee in the swanky bar of the Claridge Hotel.

Once they had ordered, Mercante got right down to business. "I promised Perón I would take care of Evita while he is in custody." He smoothed his Errol Flynn mustache and leaned toward Leary conspiratorially. "There is, it turns out, an army officer whose opinions are a big red flag. His name is Ramón Ybarra; he is a lieutenant, aide-de-camp to General Avalos."

Leary raised his eyebrows. "He's got a big job."

Mercante nodded. "Yes, especially now that Avalos has taken over as minister of war." He hiked his chair closer to the table and paused while the waiter put down the coffees. When the smiling man in the starched white jacket was gone, he continued. "We have known about Ybarra's animosity to the lady for some months, but now that he is in such a powerful position, we are quite concerned. And I want you to know that he attended the farewell rally, and out of uniform."

It occurred to Leary that Mercante's two main suspects were people that he and Perón would want out of the way under any circumstances. Was Mercante using Leary's investigation as a way to put a couple of powerful anti-Perónists out of action? The detective shook off the distracting thought and focused on the man across the little black-lacquered table. "Do you really think these two men who have been mouthing off about Señora Duarte mean her physical harm?"

Mercante drained his cup. "How can I say? But I think we have to assume that if one of them stabbed the girl to death, meaning to kill Evita, by now he has realized his mistake and will very likely try again. To be safe, we should get them both into custody."

"What is Evita doing in the meantime?"

"She is trying to get a writ of habeas corpus."

"So she will try to get Perón free?" Leary had started out to make a statement, but it had come out a question. "Does she think getting him out of jail will restore him to power?"

Mercante tugged on his French cuffs. He was a colonel in the army, but he had dressed as a dapper executive for this meeting. "I don't think Evita understands the implications of such things. How could she? But I must keep her safe." He took one of the little cookies they had served with the coffee and popped it into his mouth. He moved aside his fancy, starched white cuff and looked at his gold watch. "I have to go now. Please keep me abreast of your progress. I won't rest easy until both Puglisi and Ybarra are off the streets."

Leary shook Mercante's hand and went to retrieve his hat. He scratched his head before he put it on. Not much of what he had just learned made sense. On his way back to his desk, he tried to figure out what the colonel in the pin-striped suit was playing at. If Mercante and Perón had wanted to get Puglisi out of the way while Perón was still in office, they could have done it with one phone call. Why hadn't they? Even if Perón was under arrest now, Leary could not believe he was so suddenly and totally stripped of power that he couldn't call in a favor and get a recalcitrant union official spirited away. Ybarra would be a different ball of wax. Even before Avalos's recent elevation, the general had been commandant of the garrison at Campo de Mayo. It was well known that the army was split into factions. Not even Perón could have done away with a fellow officer with impunity. Now, he couldn't harm Ybarra in any way that Leary knew about. It was time to find out more about the lieutenant who went to political rallies in civvies.

With his boss's elevation, Lieutenant Ybarra would no longer be stationed thirty miles from the city. Most likely, he now worked in the Casa Rosada. Just last night, the Palacio Paz, the army's Buenos Aires headquarters, had been the scene of a debacle with students. There was an excuse in that. Leary could pay the lieutenant a visit on the pretext of investigating the death of the student Alberto Ara, whose brother he had interviewed the day Luz Garmendia was stabbed.

The file for that case had been collecting dust on his desk, relegated to a stack of impossible crimes that he could neither solve nor throw in the trash. A bumbling policeman trying to solve an insolvable murder, spurred by the political clout of some weepy old grandpa, might be able to elicit information Ybarra would otherwise withhold.

When Leary got to police headquarters he looked for and found a photo of Ybarra in the files. Then he picked up the Ara folder, turned right around, and headed for the Casa Rosada.

At ten that overcast morning, Ramón Ybarra saluted smartly as he as took his leave of President Fárrell and General Avalos. Things were going exactly as he'd hoped, for a change. The disarray of the various factions striving to form a new government meant that no group but the army was strong enough to take over the country. The bumbling of Fárrell and Avalos would make doubly sure this would be the case. With one Byzantine scheme weaker than the next, they went on trying to put together a new cabinet, drawing up blueprints for little piggy houses of straw and sticks. Only the army's house was built of stuff strong enough to prevail against the wolves of the left and the army's own loose canon, Perón. But Juancito was now in jail. At last. And if he could be kept there and if Fárrell and Avalos's old-man attempts to restore order failed, as they certainly would, younger officers were ready to use the army's weapons to do so. When they did, they would return Argentina to the glory days of the twenties, the decade of

Ybarra's birth, when riches had flowed into the country and, thanks to the army, order had reigned.

As he exited the Casa Rosada, Ybarra took his military cap from under his arm and was in the act of placing it on his head when a nicely dressed man of about his own age approached him on the steps. He wore a brown fedora that was too warm for the day; he carried a file folder. Another huge mob of students shouted and stamped in the road in front of the government palace.

"Excuse me, sir," the man said. "Are you Lieutenant Ramón Ybarra, the aide-de-camp to General Avalos?"

Ybarra could barely make out the man's words over the roar of the crowd chanting in the plaza behind him. "May I know who wants to know?" Ybarra had to shout to be heard, so his voice came out appropriately commanding.

The man tipped his hat. "Roberto Leary from the Federal Police." He held up the manila folder in his fist. He pointed over his shoulder at the demonstrators. "I am investigating crimes among the student protestors."

"Students, you say? Is this about the gun battle at the Palacio Paz last night?"

Leary stepped forward. "Perhaps we could stand inside the lobby for a minute to get away from this noise?"

Ybarra checked Leary's identification before he took him past a row of soldiers dressed in khaki and holding rifles that stood guard between the seat of the government and the mob in the street.

The three-story-high square entrance hall was dim, lit

only by ornamental sconces; the skylight offered only weak gray illumination on this cloudy day.

"Thank you," Leary said over the now-muffled chanting. "This is much better. I am so sorry to bother you with this matter."

"Get on with it," Ybarra said.

Leary regarded the man. Without his military cap he looked like an aristocratic portrait from the last century, with bushy dark eyebrows and the leonine forehead of a man who was too smart for his own good. "I'll try to be brief," Leary said. "A young student named Alberto Ara was shot from a speeding car during a student demonstration last week. It seems the shooter had a machine gun, and since the army owns all the machine guns that we know about—"

Ybarra interrupted him. "Of all the things that are going on this country at this moment, you have time for this? That's absurd. I myself don't have a moment for such trivialities." Ybarra started to move away, but the detective blocked his path.

"I know. I know. Just give me a couple of minutes."

Something sincere and apologetic in Leary's dark eyes made Ybarra want to take pity on the fellow. If he hadn't been in such a good mood when the cop approached him, he would not have given him ten seconds. "Get to the point."

Leary brushed his sand-colored hair off his forehead and smiled. "Thank you. I know it's stupid to think this can be solved, but the dead kid's grandfather has some pull with my boss, and I have to at least make a show of trying. I just got promoted to detective. I waited two years to get here. I don't want to get busted for not asking you."

Ybarra knew what it was like to have to wait too long for a promotion in rank. Sympathy overwhelmed his irritation at this intrusion. "Ask your question then," he said.

Leary took out a notebook and asked a couple of innocuous questions about machine guns and who had them. He wrote down some notes with a stub of pencil that looked as if it had been run over by a tank. "This is great. I can write a report that will make the poor old *abuelo* think we've tried to find out who killed his grandson." He looked up with real gratitude in his eyes. He gestured toward the door and the milling, chanting mob outside. "What do you think is going to become of all that?"

"The army will put down the chaos," Ybarra answered. "We are the only ones who can." When his plans came to fruition, it would be with tanks and more of those machine guns Leary had described.

Leary nodded. "The unions are stirring. If they come out on the other side of the question from that crowd out there, we could see a lot of trouble. Do you think they will? I hope they don't. I have a buddy on the force who says that now that Perón is jail, his actress lady friend will stir up the workers by talking on the radio."

"Not on the radio," Ybarra said. "That is no longer a possibility for her. We have seen to that." He put his hat on and started for the door. "Be prepared," he said to Leary. "It is going to take a lot of work to maintain law and order in the next couple of weeks, especially with those *cabecitas negras* from down south of the city. Those little brown people are dangerous. Some people think they'll stay in their *villas miserias* down in the suburbs. We have to make sure they do."

Leary hurried after him. He knew from Mercante's description what Ybarra's opinions supposedly were. But that was all second- and third-hand stuff. Having failed by stealth to engage Ybarra on the subject of the actress, he felt he had no choice but to tell the lieutenant about the murder case and see how he reacted. "A girl who could have been mistaken for Eva Duarte was stabbed to death a few days ago."

It stunned Leary when Ybarra said, "Oh, yes, I heard about that from General Avalos."

"How come the minister of war is taking an interest in the murder of a little nobody like Luz Garmendia?" The question was out of Leary's mouth before he considered whether it was politic to ask such a thing.

"As you can imagine," Ybarra said, "the general is keeping tabs on anything that can contribute to the uproar in the country. We heard there was a theory that the girl was murdered because she was mistaken for Perón's actress. That made it of interest." Now that Ybarra had his hat on, Leary could no longer see his eyes to tell his mood.

"Do you think that could be?" Leary asked, and waited. The yelling in the plaza was louder here near the door. *"Constitución. Constitución,"* they were calling outside.

When Ybarra didn't answer him, Leary pressed his point:

"The dead girl was last seen alive at Perón's farewell speech. I understand you were there."

"Yes, I was. So were ten or fifteen thousand other people."

Leary conceded the point. His other prime suspect, Tulio Puglisi, had also been there, as apparently had the dead girl's father and ex-boyfriend. "I think whoever killed her followed her from that rally."

Ybarra gave Leary a quizzical look. "Listen," he said, "there is part of me that wants to get mad at you, to remind you that since June we have had insanity in the capital, people marching in the streets, people throwing rocks at one another, firing machine guns from speeding cars. And you are bothering me with this stupid little murder."

Leary was getting more and more suspicious. Ybarra was too good at this game of cat and mouse and was trying too hard to deflect the questions. He could not be totally innocent of knowledge concerning the crime. "Well, I could say what an army guy would probably say, 'I'm just following orders.'"

"I suppose. But I have another theory. Have you considered that Perón might be behind the killing of the girl?"

Leary was flabbergasted. "What could be his motive?"

"Well, if she was mistaken for the actress, the dead girl must have been young, slender, and small. That's Peron's type. She looked like the actress, who looks like a sixteen-year-old herself, right? Perón has a disgusting penchant for little girls. If he had a liaison with the dead girl, he might have had her killed if he thought she was going to talk about it. You should work on that angle—that Perón raped her and had her killed because she threatened to expose him."

Leary could not speak. He had been over this with Claudia Robles's father. When the old man brought it up, Leary had figured it for senile ramblings. Was he supposed to take it seriously when it came from this powerfully connected army officer? Where could go he with such a theory? His chief would throw him out if he raised such a fantasy. Even if it might be true. "I suppose," was all he could say.

"Think about it," Ybarra said, and went out, past the guards into air thick with the shouts of the protesters.

Leary did not move for several seconds. Though he knew it might have some validity, his mind rejected the idea that in the midst of fighting for his political life Perón had found time for a dalliance with a kid and then stabbed, or had her stabbed, to death. He focused on his own theory and on Ybarra and Puglisi. One of them, or someone very like them, killed the girl, he was sure. If not, then the *modista* or the seamstress was right and either Garmendia or Torres was guilty. Any of Leary's suspects was a more plausible murderer than Juan Perón. This last possibility was not only far-fetched; it defied investigation. Then again, in this city in turmoil, how was he supposed to pursue any line of investigation?

A thought suddenly occurred to him that all but erased Perón as a possibility. From everything Leary had heard from Pilar Borelli, more than wanting to be like Evita Duarte, the Garmendia girl had wanted to *be* Evita. Luz had already had one lover. If Perón had come sniffing around, she just as likely would have willingly slept with him, and he would have nothing to fear from her. To be like her idol Evita, she would be loyal to him.

Leary went out into the noisy plaza and marched away to a beat provided by the students and well-dressed bourgeois young lawyers and bank clerks, who stamped and clapped and demanded the restoration of the constitution, which no one had paid much mind to for several decades.

The woman at the center of Leary's investigative theory was, at the moment, being invited to take a chair in the messy office of the lawyer Attilio Bramuglia. Evita was in pursuit of legal means to get her lover released from his damp jail on Martín García. The lawyer sat with his back to a rolltop desk covered with piled-up papers, facing a huge table similarly loaded with legal briefs.

The actress perched on a heavy wooden armchair across from him, the only empty seat available. Askew stacks of file folders filled all the other chairs in the room and lay on the floor all around the portly lawyer.

Evita tried to look into his eyes, but his eyeglasses reflected the glare of a fluted glass lamp hanging over his head. "You must apply for a writ of habeas corpus," she pleaded.

Bramuglia took off his spectacles and polished them with his tie. "I don't think that's the right approach right now."

She blew out an exasperated breath. "You have to. He is in prison in that miserable place. Where is your heart?" Evita's normally high-pitched voice was at the level of a screeching hawk.

"Stop that shouting!" Bramuglia scolded her as if he had the right.

Evita sputtered. She wanted to snatch up the wooden tray full of notebooks in front of her and smash him over the head with it.

He stood up and patted the air between them. "Get ahold of yourself. This is not about you. The fate of the country is at stake. Stop thinking that what happens to you is the most important issue in Argentina. The nation needs Perón to stay here, not to flee like some escaped pickpocket."

Her heart thudded against her ribs. She squeezed her lips together not to let a curse escape.

He looked directly into her eyes. It felt as if he was reading her soul. "You may become very important one day. But you are not important yet." He came to the chair next to her, took a pile of folders off it, and loaded them precariously onto a stack against the wall. "You don't know the first thing about the real issues here."

"I know what's good for Perón!" She was yelling at him, but she did not care. Mercante had said that Bramuglia was Perón's man. He was not, as far as she could see.

He looked at her as if he, too, was on the verge of violence. But he took a deep breath. "In situations like this, the only way we can get such a writ is for Colonel Perón to send a registered telegram promising to be out of the country within twenty-four hours of his release. It will be quid pro quo." He spoke as if to an unruly child.

Evita did not know the words he had said, but their meaning was obvious, and she hated it. To fight was her instinct. To lash out at the smug officers, the overfed tycoons, and especially the hypocritical church hierarchy who fathered bastards of their own and still condemned anyone born out of wedlock. All those worms wanted to keep Perón down. She swallowed her bile and implored the lawyer. "But Perón himself wants to go. I would prefer it if he would fight back. But the colonel told me himself he wants to take me away where we can live a quiet life."

Bramuglia's smile communicated disbelief bordering on mirth. "Do you really think that sentiment will stick?" He answered his own question. "Perón knows very well that if he leaves now he will never be allowed to return. I know him. He will not accept such terms."

Evita prickled at his patronizing attitude. "I doubt you know him better than I do," she said, sitting up as straight and tall as she could. This walrus of a man thought that, because she was small and a woman, he could treat her like a child. Evita looked down at her red fingernails and thought about scratching his eyes out. "He spoke his heart to me. I know what he wants."

The lawyer turned up his heavy lips in a falsely sympathetic smile. "Even if he is momentarily clinging to the idea of escape, we have to save him from himself. He is taking the path of least resistance at this point, but that will get us absolutely nowhere. I tell you Argentina needs him to stay and fight."

Stay and fight was what her heart said, too. But Perón was so vague about what he really wanted. She felt on a teeter-totter with him. One moment he seemed to be drawing her into the fray and the next pushing her to the sidelines. The people closest to him often pressed her in opposite directions. Did they understand what he wanted or were they as confused as she? They all hailed him as a great leader, but he had a strange, elusive way of ruling. "Does he have a chance to regain his position if he stays?" she asked. She did not know for sure what her colonel really wanted, but she would do anything to help his return to power.

Bramuglia shifted his weight to face her. The chair beneath him creaked. "He is walking a line between resistance and capitulation. But he must decide. I do not understand moderation in this context. There is no middle ground for me. He is essential to the nation. If he does not fight now, he will not get another chance. I think you agree, don't you?"

She looked at him, this massive man. It would take four of her to make one of him. He thought himself far superior to her, but she would not be bested in her support for Perón. "I have nothing but venom for the people who have robbed him of his position."

"Well then, there will be no writ of habeas corpus. Do you understand?"

She nodded. "But then what will we do. We cannot let him rot in jail."

This time Bramuglia's smile was pure sunshine. "We have to appeal to his supporters. If the thousands of people who love him grow to realize the overwhelming nature of their enormous numbers, nothing will stop them."

"What can I do? I am not even his wife. They have barred me from the radio. I got a call from the station head." She had been fired while Perón was with the president, signing his resignation. She wanted the microphone, wished for the hot and stuffy sound booth where she could woo the people in their kitchens and parlors, send her voice to them and make them feel what she felt. But that door was locked against her. "What can I do?" she demanded of Bramuglia again.

"You can be an inspiration," he said. "That will be enough. You shout too much. You are the kind of person who can whisper and be heard. Stop shouting."

While Evita ruminated about the true meaning of Bramuglia's advice, the crowd in the plaza in front of the Casa Rosada became bolder and bolder. The day wore on and the setting sun reflected its fire in the windows of the seat of government. President Fárrell discussed who might be appointed to a new cabinet and dwelled on the problem of Perón and how to muzzle him for good, and the leftist demonstrators outside in the square became more and more unruly.

Ybarra, sitting in on a meeting in the office of the paper-tiger president, did his best not to smirk. His plan was going to work despite the so-so news from Francisco Rocco. No one above the rank of captain had agreed to join them. But a couple of captains were solidly with them. The army had risen up with only junior officers before. It could again. Ybarra had drawn up a detailed plan for how the troops from the Campo de Mayo would march on the center and put down the rabble. "If we don't fight back now, we will lose the country for a long time," he blurted out, giving voice to his inner thoughts despite himself.

General Avalos looked annoyed and remained cautious. "Without Perón, the army has no civilian constituency," he said. "We must legitimize our position. That means forming a government that can attract adherents among the powerful outside the military."

Ybarra let him blather on. The army's tanks and guns would soon be commanded by men with the balls to use them. Ybarra chewed on his thumb. He needed to be more careful about what he said. If he and his comrades declared themselves too soon, they would wind up in the brig, probably for the rest of their short lives. He would see the proper moment when it arrived, when Fárrell and Avalos were done for and before Perón had risen from the dead.

President Fárrell gave Ybarra an arch look. "My boy," he said, "stop scowling. I know well your point of view, but Perón is marginal and inconsequential at this point. No one but us knows where he is. I will send out a communiqué say-

ing that he is not in jail, and that will convince his supporters that he has abandoned them."

The crowd on the streets soon proved Fárrell wrong. Late
that afternoon, shooting began within a block of the Casa
Rosada. Pro-Perón protestors staged a raid on the officer's
club at the Palacio Paz. Pistol shots popped back and forth
between the demonstrators and the military men inside. At
one point someone went to the roof of the Palacio Paz with
a machine gun. As shots sputtered down into the street, forty
mounted policemen attacked the protestors from the rear,
plunging their horses into the crowd and swinging their
sabers at medical students and middle-level bureaucrats in
cheap suits. The crowd scattered through the streets, shouting
slogans. Some of the unruly and frustrated demonstrators
sniped at the police from behind barricades in darkened door-
ways. It would be midnight before the tumult subsided. By
then a prominent physician would be killed and the hospitals
would have filled up with nearly two score wounded.

As the riot was heating up, Evita returned to Pierina
Dealessi's apartment from her meeting with Bramuglia.
Pierina lived in a turn-of-the-century Belle Epoque building. The french doors of the facade had little wrought-iron
balustrades, and when the windows were opened they made
little balconies where a child such as Evita had been might
dream of reciting poetry to a crowd down in the street. When
Evita entered the apartment, she discovered that her friend
was still at the Teatro Nacional Cervantes, rehearsing her new
play. Though Evita knew well the tradition of the theater, it

still amazed her that entertainments were being planned while people were being killed in the plazas. She took one of Pierina's chic but uncomfortable Art Deco chairs and phoned home to find out what news there was of her colonel. Cristina answered the phone. Her radio was blaring a bolero in the background.

"Señora," she said, her voice pitched to fear level, "some soldiers came. They have taken Domingo Mercante. He told Jorge to tell you that he is going to jail. Jorge says he will take Señor Mercante's place as your protector."

"Is Jorge there?"

"No, señora. He went to get a car for you because the government men came to take away the Packard. Señor Mercante is going to give you his Chevrolet. Jorge went to get it and bring it to you."

"Good," Evita said.

"Señora, I am afraid."

"Oh, Cristina. Just stay inside. You will have nothing to fear if you stay off the streets. We left a good deal of food there. Just don't go out."

"No, señora. Not for me. I'm afraid for you. It is that Jorge—he is very short and skinny. He will not be able to protect you now that Domingo Mercante has been taken away."

That evening, a special edition of *Crítica*, the mostly widely circulated news daily in Argentina, announced in a banner front-page headline, PERÓN NO LONGER A THREAT TO THE COUNTRY.

While Eva Duarte was on the phone with her housekeeper, Lieutenant Ramón Ybarra at the besieged officer's club in the Palacio Paz and Tulio Puglisi in the office of the National Shoe Makers Union both read the headline, smacked it, and uttered the same oath: "Not if that bitch of an actress can stir up the *descamisados.*" Ybarra imagined the treads of tanks rolling over the cobblestones of the center to prevent that from happening. He already knew which streets and avenues they would take. Puglisi imagined the poor slobs by the thousands hailing Perón and wondered what the defeated people in Italy and Germany would think when they saw films of Argentine fascist rallies on their newsreels.

When Evita hung up on her housekeeper, she took her goose-fleshed body to the window, grateful that it was covered with wrought iron. The grating gave a decorative air to the facade of the building but its real purpose was to keep out thieves. Perhaps it would also bar a man who might come to kill the mistress of Juan Perón.

Someone had already killed little Luz just for looking like Eva Duarte.

Evita thought about the last time she had seen the girl at the *modista*'s shop just before Perón's fiftieth birthday party. They had all joked about Evita's new ensemble of matching silk pants and shirt, very like those they had seen in films with Katharine Hepburn. She had given Luz one of her cast-off dresses that day—a cute green one. There had been tears of gratitude in Luz's eyes. She had taken the dress tenderly, as if it were a piece of rare porcelain, and brought it into the dressing room and tried it on. Now the police thought she had died because she resembled Eva the actress.

Evita saw herself reflected in the window before her. Luz had looked like her in that dress, but she had not been like her. Luz was soft all the way through. Evita knew she had a will of steel inside her.

Bramuglia had said she could whisper and save Perón, but she could not feel that way at the moment. All she could think to say right now were her prayers. For Luz. For herself.

She put her finger on the inside of the glass and traced the vine-and-leaf design of the iron grillwork outside. It seemed to her that tonight she and Juan Perón were both behind bars.

SUNDAY, OCTOBER 14

Early the next morning, with the streets of the Palermo district as quiet as on any Sunday, Jorge Webber arrived at Pierina Dealessi's building carrying a box of *medialunas* from the nearby bakery. He met Dealessi coming out the front door, taking her mother and sister to Mass. "Evita is up there," Señora Dealessi said, without preamble. "There is a military officer with her."

Jorge's nerves rang an alarm. Rather than wait for the dolt of an elevator operator, he took the marble stairs two at a time to the third floor. A military officer? It could be someone from the government to take Evita into custody. She had only him to protect her. He wished he had a gun.

He reached the apartment at a trot and stopped before the door that had been left ajar. He heard her voice. He entered decorously despite his anxiety. Evita was sitting in a chair in the corner of the salon, reading a letter. A short, stocky in man in a colonel's uniform sat on a love seat near her, under a large poster of the Paris World's Fair.

Evita looked up and smiled as she took the pastries from him. "Oh, thank you, Jorge. Now I have something nice to offer Colonel Mazza. Would you go down to the café on the corner and bring us some coffee, too?" She went back to reading the letter. Whatever it said, it made her tremble.

Evita waited until Webber had gone before she spoke to the polite and elegant man opposite her. Miguel Angel Mazza was an army surgeon who wore the uniform of a colonel, the only symbol of the army she could stomach, because it was the uniform Perón had been wearing when she met him. "Tell me how he seemed when you saw him?" she asked.

"Subdued," Mazza said. "But he is well. We think we can make a case to bring him back to Buenos Aires. He will still be in custody, but at least we can get him off that dreadful island."

She moved next to him on the love seat. Perón's letter had lifted her heart but roiled her mind. "Is there anything I can do to help?" She told him about her visit to Bramuglia and his refusal even to try to get the writ of habeas corpus.

"I have heard about that," Mazza said. "You are assuming Perón really wants to leave the country and retire from politics."

"It says that in this letter you just brought to me." She tapped her nails on the paper in her lap.

"I do not know what he said to you, señora. But I don't think he has made a final decision about what he will do. You know he always plays his cards close to his vest. I think he wants to keep all paths open."

She did know how secretive he could be. He had said it himself once when speaking of his underlings in the government. "Often," he had told her, "it is best for the person in charge to watch how a situation plays out and to step in at the last moment to embrace victory or disclaim defeat." She had thought Perón so wise when he said that. But she feared she was now on the receiving end of that same strategy. Clinging to Perón was where her future lay. Without him, where would she go? When they took him away, he had said he wanted her to stand by him, but how could she, if she didn't know where he stood?

As if to prove her point, Mazza opened the dark leather case in which he had carried Perón's letter to her—the first love letter she had ever had from anyone. Mazza took out another envelope, identical to the one she had received. "When I leave you, I am going to deliver this to the editor of *La Prensa*."

Evita took it. It was unsealed. She removed a second letter written on paper like that of Perón's letter to her and also in his own hand. "Open letter to President Edelmiro Fárrell," it said at the top. Evita scanned it quickly. Perón was publicly demanding to be put on trial or to be returned to his previous status. These demands belied the soul he bared in what he had written to her.

Which were his real sentiments? He had told her he was finished with political life. This public statement said he expected to be given his freedom to participate in governing Argentina. She did not know where her mind should go.

She chewed on her index finger. Her heart was split in two. A little voice in a dark corner of her mind warned her that she should distrust Perón for not telling her the truth of his feelings. It said he did not trust her, that he did not think her strong enough or brave enough to do anything useful. Otherwise, he would have been calling on her to fight for him. She wanted him to be again the powerful man he was when they met. It seemed impossible that Perón could fade from the halls of government in a few days and leave nothing behind, less than the wake of that small boat that had brought her back to Buenos Aires from Tres Bocas.

His letter to her offered a peaceful life away from all the political uproar. The idea was seductive. She was tired. She had been anemic for so long. It made her listless, made her long for a life of leisure. But under that fatigue she felt a reservoir of boiling anger that fed her determination and made her want to defeat those who would put Perón down, who would rob him of his rightful place, and rob her of the chance to become the woman she was destined to be.

"What do you think will happen next?" she asked Mazza.

He gazed at her with kind eyes and took her hand. His was warm and soft, the hand of a doctor, not a soldier. "Some small pro-Perón rallies have started up here and there," he said, "but so far they don't carry enough weight. Fárrell is keeping Perón's whereabouts a secret. As long as the workers don't know where he is, they may think he just went away."

Evita longed again for the sound booth. She had spent the last two years talking into Radio Belgrano's shiny round microphones, pretending to be the most important women of history: Catherine the Great of Russia, Elizabeth of England, and Eliza Lynch of Paraguay, who like Evita was not married to her man but helped to make him great. If only she could broadcast the news the laborers needed to hear, she could make them see the role they must now play. She had to find a way to show Perón she could be brave and strong and useful.

"I think Bramuglia is right," she said at last. "We have to stay and fight. Perón cannot abandon everything he has worked for all these years. Did you know that I met him when he was raising funds for the poor victims of the earthquake in San Juan? Our first experience together was in an effort to help the unfortunate. Perón must be restored to his rightful place." By the time she finished speaking, she was up and pacing Pierina's blue-and-white Chinese carpet.

Webber came back and put a tray of coffees on the low table in front of the love seat.

Mazza smiled approvingly at her as she drank her espresso. He stood and kissed her cheek. "I must go now and deliver Perón's letter to *La Prensa*."

After he had gone, she sat and read again the most beautiful phrases from Perón's letter to her. "My adored treasure . . . Now I know how much I love you . . . as soon as I get out, we'll get married and go somewhere and live peacefully . . . love me very much because I need your love more than ever . . . Many, many kisses to my dearest *chinita*. Perón."

She kissed his signature. These were words of commitment to her. But in many ways, they were the sentiments of a man defeated. A man who wanted to escape from everything with the woman he adored. Twice on this page he had mentioned retirement. The exact opposite of the public letter Mazza was on his way to deliver.

She nibbled on a pastry and wondered why going away with Perón and living a small, pleasant life was not enough for her, a girl who had risen from poverty, who had pushed herself to where she was with only the strength in this small body. But her very bone marrow refused to settle for what her mother had wanted for her and what her sisters wanted for themselves. To be a conventional wife was all they had ever longed for: the small satisfactions of normal domesticity. Evita could not help it. They were not enough for her. They never would be.

Perón's letter also spoke of the anger in his heart: "What do you think of Fárrell and Avalos? A couple of bastards doing that to their friend . . . Be very calm. Mazza will tell you how everything stands . . . The evil of this time and especially of this country is the existence of all these idiots, and you know that an idiot is worse than a villain . . ."

She wanted to slap the faces of those idiots who were, to her, both stupid and villainous.

Even in this love letter, Perón spoke of the wrongs that had been done to him, as if he were calling on her love to redress them. She kissed his signature again and put the letter in her purse.

Jorge Webber came back into the salon and made a show of clearing away the tray.

"Turn on the radio, please, Jorge," she said. "Let's see if there is any news."

He twisted the dial of the tall radio that stood in the corner but found only a Mass from the cathedral, some operatic arias, and a sports announcer talking about soccer.

"Switch it off," she said. Her resolve rose and faded by turns.

As if he read her thoughts, the chauffeur spoke. "It has to be you, señora, who makes the appeal to the workers. You are the only one who can save him now."

Evita opened her mouth to put him in his place, but at that moment Pierina Dealessi returned from church. "Save who from what?" she asked Evita. She took off her hat and replaced her hat pin in the crown. She pulled off her mink stole, made from whole-animal pelts including the heads with little beady eyes, and handed it to Jorge, along with the hat and her long black gloves, as if he were her personal valet.

"Save Perón from that awful jail," Evita said. "People think I can do something to change matters. I keep telling them I can't. I am not even his wife. And he can never marry a nobody like me."

Pierina laughed. "He will marry you. I swear he will," she said. With a flick of her slender fingers, she shooed Webber away.

Biting back resentment, he took her things out but quickly returned. With Mercante in jail, he was the one who was supposed to take care of Evita. When he reentered the room, the Dealessi woman was already sitting on the love seat with Evita, their heads together.

". . . The circumstances of my birth—" Evita was saying. "Those tepid army officers don't understand love. They would never accept such a marriage. They call me the colonel's folly."

"Nevertheless, he will do it." Dealessi picked up a pastry from the dish before her, took one bite, and threw the rest back on the tray.

"Why do you think so?" Evita's tone seemed to beg for reassurance.

Pierina laughed. "Because, although you don't make much of an impression on the stage, darling, every day you portray to the world an image of Eva Duarte that you have written for yourself—you have stopped being that desperate little girl I first met, starving and doing anything to get even the smallest part. Now you sit with powerful men and act as if you have a right to give them your opinions. In real life, your performance is absolutely compelling."

Evita looked at her friend in wonder, as if she had revealed some biblical truth. Neither of them spoke for a moment. A decision blurted out of Evita's mouth before she was sure she had made it: "I have to help restore him to power. If I go to the barrios and talk to the *descamisados,* the poor workers will see they must stand up for the only person in power who ever gave them a single thought. All they need is someone to tell them what to do." She was positive in her heart that she, more than anyone else, could make it work.

"They will believe you because at heart you are one of them," Pierina said.

A fear Pierina did not understand flickered in Evita's eyes. "What gives you pause, Eva?"

Evita shook her head. "Yesterday, the lawyer Bramuglia said I can whisper and be heard, and Colonel Miguel Angel Mazza encouraged me right here less than half an hour ago. But Perón . . ." She hesitated. She wanted to confess that she was not sure Perón trusted her to do the right thing. But she shrank from saying it aloud and making it true. "Isn't it interesting that Mazza's name is Angel?" she said instead. She looked at Dealessi expectantly, as if she wanted her friend to believe that Mazza was a messenger from heaven—like the angel Gabriel at the Annunciation.

"Well, if you ask me," Pierina said, "some leadership is required. Low-level people always need someone to tell them what to do."

Evita's dark eyes shone. "That's what people always think about the poor." She turned to Webber, who was standing at attention in the corner, like some medieval page. "Do you have Mercante's car nearby?" she asked him.

"Yes, I can have it out front in a few minutes," he said.

"Bring it around, please. As long as the workers are with us, we will be unstoppable. I cannot organize them, but I can find out what they are thinking. That information may be useful to the colonel's supporters. It's time to take a ride through the barrios."

"Be careful," Dealessi said. "The situation out there is a tinderbox."

Evita thought of the death of that poor girl Luz. Mercante said the police thought she had been killed because she was mistaken for Evita. But she refused to believe it. Except for her body, the girl did not resemble her at all. Pierina did not know anything about that murder, and it was best she didn't. She would be overprotective. Evita saw no reason to fear the *descamisados*. If someone wanted to kill her for supporting Perón, he would be found in the Barrio Norte, where the oligarchy lived in their huge villas, not in the hovels that lined the streets of the working-class villages.

She put on her black straw hat, took her purse with Perón's letter in it, and went out to meet Jorge at the front door of the building.

As the chauffeur drove Mercante's gray Chevrolet sedan south toward La Boca, he warned Evita that the places where the workers lived would not be beautiful and leafy enclaves like the one she was used to. She smiled to herself. He thought she did not know how the poor lived, she who had practically starved to death while looking for work in the theater when she was just sixteen. In those days, a cup of coffee with condensed milk was like a three-course meal to her.

She took out Perón's letter and ran her fingertips over the words *only when we are separated from those we love can we know how much we love them.* She wanted him. How was she supposed to know if she was doing the right thing if she could not see it in his eyes?

As they left the narrow streets of San Telmo and entered La Boca, they passed a gasworks with huge cylindrical containers, their domed roofs at different heights, the girders above them silhouetted against the cloudy sky.

Jorge turned into a long, straight street lined with boardinghouses of the type Evita knew well. "Stop up there," she called to Jorge in the front seat. "Where those people are gathered in front of that corner store."

Seeing his chauffeur's cap in the rearview mirror warned her. "Take off your hat and don't get out of the car. Your uniform is out of place here. It will make them suspicious."

When he pulled up to the curb, Evita got out of the backseat and approached a knot of about eight people, all but one men. Two little boys were shooting marbles in a patch of dirt between the street and cracked sidewalk.

"The store is closed, señora," a young man not much taller than Evita said apologetically. "Sunday," he said, by way of explanation.

She had not thought about what she would say to them. "Yes, of course," fell from her lips. She was used to having scripts to read when she played the heroine.

They looked through the windshield at Jorge behind the wheel. No doubt, even without his cap, his chauffeur's jacket with its epaulets gave him away.

"Thank you," Evita said and retreated toward the car. Jorge started it up.

A stocky man with a soccer ball under his arm pointed at Webber. "What do these people want here?" he demanded. The others clustered around him.

Evita got in the front seat. "Drive on, Jorge," she said.

He put the car in gear and nearly hit the advancing soccer player as he pulled away. "You see," Webber said. "These are rough places."

"Perhaps I should go back to Pierina's," she said. Then she immediately rescinded. "Let's try one more."

He continued south, past the warehouses toward Avellaneda.

"We have to approach this differently," she said. "You have to take off that jacket and tie. "She took off her rings and her necklace and dropped them into her purse as she spoke. She removed her hat and tossed it into the back. She was happy in these circumstances not to have the Packard.

Jorge pulled over on a deserted stretch along the Riachuelo, the river that separated Buenos Aires from the meatpacking suburb. He got out of the car, took off his jacket and tie, and placed them, carefully folded, on the backseat. If he left the car, his jodhpurs and tall boots would give them away, but when he got back into the car, sitting down, he looked like an ordinary man through the windows.

"Drive on," she told him. She took out her letter again and reread Perón's plea for her safety. "You should keep calm and take care of your health . . ." it said. "I would be more calm if I knew you were not in danger and that you were well." What would he think if he knew where she was? she wondered. But how could he be angry with her? After more than a year and a half together, he must realize she would not remain passive. She was incapable of doing nothing.

They rode through a shantytown and entered a street lined by one-story dreary houses, the gutters filled with trash. A dirty, skinny, ill-clad child pushed the remains of a broom back and forth in a deep puddle of black water. Evita could not tell if it was a boy or a girl. This squalid place was more awful than the worst hovel where she had lived as a child. Here she would find the people who had no one but Perón. Without him, that child with the broom would never have a life any better than this.

"Stop there." She pointed across the street to an old woman sitting on a chair beside an open door. The tiny house was painted a streaky, venomous shade of green. The grandmother cradled a baby on her lap while she crocheted lace. Three young men on the sidewalk were building something un-identifiable with scraps of wood. They all looked askance at the car.

Evita got out and approached, holding out her hand to the woman. "My name is Eva," she said. "Eva Duarte."

The men stopped hammering. One who had been kneel-ing stood up. The old woman smiled. One of her front teeth was chipped and crooked. "I listened to you on the radio. *Jabón Radical*." She named the brand of soap that had been Evita's sponsor.

"Yes," Evita said and returned the woman's grin. The three men came nearer. "I just wanted people to know that Colonel Perón has been arrested. He is in jail."

"Por Dios!" one of the men exclaimed. He slapped the saw he held with the flat of his other hand. The ringing sound it made startled the baby.

The woman dropped her handiwork and stood up, moving the wailing infant to her shoulder. She patted it on the back. "It is just what I told you, Adelio." She gestured toward a man who taken nails from between his lips and now threw them and his hammer onto the cement sidewalk. "Bastards."

Evita nodded vigorously. "The president is saying it is not true. That Perón is not in jail. But I swear he is." She held up her hand as if she were speaking in court. "I know it."

"What can we do?" asked the man with the saw. It was not clear if his question was for the old woman, for Evita, or for his comrades.

"The men at the plant need to know the truth," the one called Adelio said. "As soon as our shift starts at midnight."

"Yes, pass the word," Evita said. "Pass the word." She shook hands with them, kissed the now quiet baby on the back of its head. "Your grandchild is beautiful," she said.

"He is my son," the woman said.

Evita bowed her head in embarrassment and returned to the car.

They spent the afternoon stopping here and there in Barracas, Parque Patricios, Berisso, wherever they saw a small group gathered on the streets or in the plazas on that muggy, overcast Sunday afternoon.

Between stops, Evita thought about the suffering of that woman who looked twice her age and read Perón's letter over and over again and convinced herself that, despite what he'd said, he would prefer her to be doing this. He had to. For the sake of that woman and her baby and the little child playing with the broom in the putrid water.

All day she listened to the workers tell of their outrage over Perón's having been deposed. The same scene replayed at each stop. When she told the poor laborers that Perón had been jailed, they cursed and excused themselves for taking the Lord's name in vain in front of a lady. When they asked her what to do, she told them to make sure that their co-workers knew about their hero's incarceration.

Inside the car, Perón's letter told her he wanted peace, not responsibility. Each time she got out of the car, she reminded herself of his open letter to the president. Somewhere in all this was her future. She wanted it to be one in which she had his full confidence. Then she would fly like a hawk, swoop at the people who blocked Perón from helping the poor. She pictured a bird tearing out the throats of those disgusting oligarchs who looked down on her.

"These are dangerous days," one poor worker's wife told her. "People are already dying in the streets in the center." The practically toothless woman had only one son and was terrified of losing him to a stray bullet from a speeding car.

Without thinking twice, Evita put her hand on the woman's shoulder and said, "More people may die. Many could die, but it is more painful to die of hunger than of bullets or the knife." She kept her face determined, but her heart trembled with the thought that she could die in such a way herself. As Luz had.

In the city center, a tenuous order was maintained by the mounted police clattering along the side streets with World War I vintage Mauser rifles slung over their shoulders. The weapons were out-of-date and some citizens laughed at them, but others reminded their companions that shots from passé guns could still tear holes in people.

The clouds broke in midafternoon, but the mood of Buenos Aires did not brighten. On the broad avenues, carabineers by the truckload rolled up and down past tense citizens who looked the other way and prayed they could make it to wherever they were going without being wounded. Or worse. Sentries marched before the major government buildings as if they were doing guard duty in a war zone.

Roberto Leary entered the offices of the National Shoe Workers Union, where the officials of several syndicates had eschewed observing the day of rest in order to meet and plan their strategy.

Leaving the blinding spring sunlight in the empty street outside, the detective found a room as dark as a movie theater. The windows were covered over with black cloth, as if they were in London during the Blitz. Gooseneck lamps shone pools of light on a dozen or so gray metal desks lined up in three rows. A cloud of cigarette smoke hovered over the green glass shades. Leary found Tulio Puglisi banging his hand on the headline that said Perón was no longer a danger to the nation and haranguing three other union officials gathered around him.

The man was obviously a hothead.

Leary approached and told Puglisi he needed to ask him a few questions. Puglisi grabbed his hat and jacket and led the detective to the deserted café on the corner. "It's a dump," he said, "but the coffee is first rate."

On the way, Puglisi ranted about the actress and the stupidity of the other unionists. "Mine and the Textile Workers are the only unions that get it. How can real union leaders support a fascist? I know Perón has bought off his loyalists with good jobs for their brothers and cousins. But I don't see what the rest of the labor men can be thinking. Perón is importing the butchers of Europe. Don't those jerks who stick with him read the papers? Do they even look at the pictures? Or the newsreels? Do they see what the fascist war did to Europe? Have they looked at the eyes in those photographs of starved wraiths who survived the death camps? People over there are walking around in bombed-out cities, surrounded by rubble, desperate for something to eat. Even the winners. Do they want that to happen here?"

Leary did not respond. He let Puglisi rage on. But he had to admit that a lot of what he said made sense. Then again, even a murderer could make sense and still be guilty.

The café where Tulio brought him had certainly seen better days. Paneling of scratched and battered dark wood and a floor of cracked and broken terra-cotta tiles had once had pretenses toward class, but they had seen too much rough treatment to retain any of their initial beauty. Once Puglisi and Leary were standing at the beat-up zinc-topped bar, Leary tried to think of the best opening gambit for what he wanted to ask. He sipped his coffee. It was really good, great even. "I wasn't at Perón's farewell rally on Wednesday, but I heard you were there."

"What a lot a bullshit that was," Puglisi said and drained his cup.

Leary turned his back on the barista who had lowered the radio broadcast of a Boca Juniors soccer game and was taking too much of an interest in the conversation. "There was a girl at the rally, in a green dress, who looked like Eva Duarte," he said quietly. "I was wondering if you saw her."

Puglisi answered immediately, without moderating his usually loud tone. "Yeah, I saw her. I thought it was kind of funny that the actress was in the middle of the crowd and not with the bigwigs near the platform. I followed her for a block or two before I saw that the girl wasn't the colonel's lady friend."

"What did you do when you realized that?" Leary asked.

"I went home and consoled myself by making love to my wife. Why are you asking me this?"

Leary decided not to say. "Why did you follow the girl? Why would you follow Eva Duarte?"

"I was curious about her."

"Curious? What did you mean to do to her?"

"Nothing," Puglisi protested in that trumpet voice of his. "I wanted to see if Evita would start rabble-rousing among the workers. Trying to get them to march on the Casa Rosada to restore Perón. Something like that." He looked insulted but also unsure that Leary would believe him.

"Look, Tulio, I heard what you said about Eva Duarte last week. I want to know if you followed the girl because you meant Eva Duarte harm."

Puglisi laughed out loud. "Me? Harm her? You ought to be following her to see what harm she is likely to do to Argentina." He looked at Leary's eyes, and the smile disappeared from his face. "Why exactly are you so interested in all of this?" he asked in all seriousness.

Leary handed a few coins to the nosy barista to pay for the coffees and walked toward the door. When they were out of earshot, he told Puglisi the truth. "The girl you mistook for Eva Duarte was stabbed to death that night. I am investigating her murder."

Puglisi's blue eyes widened. He raised his shoulders and

turned up his palms, making a very good show of being shocked and confused by the news.

Alone in her shop at six o'clock that evening, Claudia stubbed out her cigarette and threw down her sketch pad and pencil. She had been struggling all afternoon to turn her mind to something, anything but Luz's murder.

Hernán was busy at home smashing his index fingers on the keys of his Olivetti portable and muttering things like, "Bastards." And every once in a while, out of the blue, demanding her opinion of things like, "Why did they lift the state of siege only to reimpose it after less than two months?" It drove her crazy when he treated her as if she were nothing but a sponge to soak up his anger at the political situation. Her father was out playing dominoes with his cronies at their social club in the church basement.

Though it was Sunday, she had finally left home, telling Hernán she wanted to work on entering her receipts in the store ledger. He grunted and went on typing, and she took the Subte to the shop. She was already on the train when it occurred to her that she was on her way to the scene of the murder. She staved off a shudder. If Leary was right that Luz had died because she looked like Evita, Claudia was in no danger. She was three inches taller than and twenty years older than the actress. No one would mistake her for Evita.

Guilt still haunted her. She carried it with her to work and let it prevent her from ever touching her ledger book.

Instead, she sat sketching dresses and let regret drip into her heart. How could a serious woman try to think up new evening gowns under such circumstances? Did she think such trivialities could hold off her remorse? Each sketched idea brought thoughts of customers who might wear the dress, customers who were nowhere to be found in these trying times. Who might never return now that an innocent girl had been stabbed to death at the front door of Chez Claudia. The lack of their custom could mean the end of her business. That outcome seemed only just, considering that she had set in motion a course of events that led to a murder.

Around and around went her thoughts until she had no choice but to give up and go home.

She went into the little bathroom and thought again of throwing up the morning after Luz was slain. Not understanding why, she ran a powder puff over her face and daubed on a little lipstick. She put on her hat and jacket. She would rather listen to Hernán type and complain. She dialed their number to tell him she was coming home, but got no answer.

She reached him at the paper. "I came in to the office to see if there was anything happening that we might actually report," he said.

She told him she would meet him at their apartment, locked up the store, and made for the C-line toward Constitución. The Subte was slow in coming and nearly empty on a Sunday. The rattan was unraveling on the seat beside hers. The ride was boring, and she had nothing to do but brood and wish she had brought along her sketch pad.

Dusk was falling as she turned into the path leading to her building's front door. In the gloom under a thick magnolia tree, Lázaro Torres stepped in front of her with a knife in his hand.

Shock forced a gasp from her, and fear shook her knees. She burst into tears.

He flashed her a malevolent grin. "What are you crying for, bitch?" He pulled her into the alley beside the building, then pushed her through a low door into the basement. "Luz is dead," he said. "You better tell me what you know about it or else."

Hernán Mantell left the paper after eight that evening. He had wasted the day. Some union members had staged brief strikes. The union leadership was not supporting them, so the whole picture remained confused. He had spent the entire afternoon working on a piece, concluding that with Perón in jail, the Nazi–Fascist tendencies of the government would fade and now Argentina would enter an era of democracy. It might have been an exercise in wishful thinking on his part, but he hoped that putting it in print might help make it come true. And he was sure the generals would let them print something optimistic about the country's future.

His editor had scuttled the story anyway. The government was not letting them print anything that confirmed Perón was in jail. And his editor supported the president's order to keep a lid on that news. "If word gets around," he said, "the pro-Perón forces will have a field day. No, Hernán, if we want Colonel Juancito Perón to stay in the pokey, we have to keep his whereabouts a mystery to his *descamisados*."

Hernán bit his lip in front of his boss and grumbled to himself all the way home. When he parked his car and walked exhausted and disappointed to his apartment, he found the place dark. He threw his tie and jacket on a chair in the foyer and dialed the shop. There was no answer. He went down to old Gregorio's flat, where he expected Claudia had gone for company. He found her father sitting alone, reading the paper and eating scrambled eggs.

"She is not here," the old man said. "I looked for her upstairs earlier, but she wasn't there."

Of course you did, Hernán thought. She always made the old man's dinner, and if she had been at home, he would have been with her upstairs, eating something much tastier than those eggs. Hernán was worried and pissed off, but he did not want to alarm her father.

"I thought maybe the two of you had gone out to eat and forgotten to tell me," Gregorio said.

"She's probably upstairs already. She could have been going up in the elevator while I was coming down the steps." Hernán tried to keep his tone light, but now he was really concerned. Claudia had said she was on her way home over two hours ago. She never went places by herself at night, especially in times like these. And she always made sure her father knew where she was. He had given her a lot of freedom when she was a child, and as a teenager she had made sure he continued to do so by never causing him any worry. She had gone on with that habit all her life. "Don't worry," Hernán said to the old man. "I will send her down as soon as she gets home."

He went to the lobby and asked the elevator operator if he had seen her. The man hardly looked up from his sports page. "Not since she went out around noon."

Hernán sped up the three flights and found their apartment still empty. He phoned the shop again but still got no answer. He wished he had the telephone number of the seamstress, just in case she knew what was going on. But he didn't even know her last name.

When a knock came on the door an hour later, he jumped out of his chair, scared he was going to see the police outside his door. But it was her father. "I waited as long as I could," he said. "I thought if the two of you were having an argument, I should not come up. But I listened to the silence from the hall. It frightened me more than if you had been shouting threats at one another."

"I am sure she is okay," Hernán said, totally unconvincingly.

They sat together without exchanging more than a few words until ten minutes to eleven. Hernán thought the old man would fall asleep, but he did not. They tuned in the radio, but neither of them seemed to be listening to the mournful tango music. When her key turned in the door, they both jumped up instantly, their terror shaking them.

She looked exhausted. She hardly took two steps into the

room before she started unbuckling her platform shoes. Hernán remembered that she had not slept much since the girl Luz was murdered.

"I am sorry," she said, as if that were enough. As if all she had done was trod on their toes.

Hernán wanted to scream at her, but he could not do that in front of Gregorio, who just sighed and walked to her. He kissed her on the forehead and said, "I love you."

Hernán could not manage such patience. "I was scared to death. Why didn't you call?" His voice was trembling with anger and residual adrenaline.

Gregorio walked to the door. "I love you, my darling," he said and went out, closing the door without making a sound.

When the old man was out of earshot, Hernán exploded. "Answer me. Why didn't you call?"

"I couldn't."

"What is that supposed to mean?" he screamed. "There are pay phones all over the city. Your father and I were sitting here terrified, while you couldn't be bothered to tell us where you were."

She jumped up and ran into the bathroom and slammed the door.

He ran and tried to stop her, but the door was closed and locked by the time he got there. He pounded on it.

"Go away," she shouted. "Just go away."

"Claudia, stop it." He turned the knob and banged on the door some more.

He shouted for a minute and then began to plead and then scold again. On the other side of the door, Claudia put her fingers in her ears and ran the bath water to drown him out.

When he got no response from her, he shouted, "The hell with this," went into the bedroom, and slammed the door. He waited for her to come in, thinking of the things he planned to say to her: to tell her she had frightened her poor old father. How if she didn't care for him, she should at least be courteous to the man who had devoted his life to raising her. To tell her how difficult it had been to sit there with her father, knowing that both of them had imagined her stabbed to death as Luz had been. He stripped to his boxers and threw himself on the bed, rehearsing a vicious scolding in his mind. He fell asleep before he got a chance to deliver it.

MONDAY, OCTOBER 15

In the blue light of early dawn, Hernán found Claudia wearing only her slip, asleep on the couch. As soon as he opened the door, she sat up.

"Please forgive me," he said. "Please. I am sorry I got mad at you. But I had been so worried."

Her thick, dark brown hair, which she always wore in a chignon, had tumbled down around her shoulders. Bobby pins were scattered on the floor. There were black circles under her eyes.

She did not want to forgive him, but she could not find her anger from the night before.

He sat beside her. "Tell me what happened, exactly," he said softly.

"Lázaro Torres."

"The gardener?" Alarm turned the skin of his back to ice.

She nodded. "He pulled a knife on me."

"*What?*" Hernán shouted at the top of his voice.

"I was on the path coming to the downstairs door. He took a switchblade out of his pocket and dragged me into the basement—that room where he keeps his rakes and wheelbarrow."

Hernán leaped to his feet. "Good God! Why didn't you tell me this last night?" He did not wait for an answer. He ran into the bedroom and pulled on a pair of trousers and shoved his feet into his loafers. He went to the apartment door like a streak.

She ran and tried to block him. "*No!* He will hurt you."

"You are crazy for not telling me this before." He pushed past her and ran down the stairs, jumping down the last three steps to each landing. When he got to the basement door, it was open. It was still dark in the narrow alley. His heart pounding, he reached in and groped for the light switch. Why hadn't he brought a kitchen knife with him?

His fingers found the switch on the right wall beside the doorjamb. When the light came on, the room was empty. He ran out to the street. There was no sign of the son of bitch out on the block.

When he got back to their apartment, Claudia, still in her slip, was standing in the open doorway. "He's gone," Hernán said. He led her inside and sat beside her on the sofa. "Tell me the whole story."

"He was drunk. He brandished a piece from the newspaper

at me. He said he was sure I knew where Luz had gone when she ran away from him. He said what I have been thinking: that if she had stayed with him, she would still be alive. He wept. Her father wept the same way."

"Her father was there?"

"No. A couple of days ago I went to pay a condolence call on him and her grandmother."

"You what? You are nuts! I like to think of you as an artist, a creative type who's more intuitive than logical, but Jesus Christ, Claudia! Have you no sense? One of those brutes must have killed that poor girl and you are paying social calls on them?" He was shouting so loud it hurt her ears.

She began to weep. "I did not pay a social call on Torres," she said. "He forced me into that filthy room. He made me confess that I was the one who took her away from him. He kept drinking from a bottle of aguardiente he pulled out of an old watering can. He spat at me. He threatened me with his knife. I was sure I was going to die the way she did." She could not continue.

Hernán took her in his arms and put his hand on the back of her head.

"He told me it was my fault that Luz was murdered. And he was right." She sobbed so deeply that it took her a moment to catch enough breath to speak. "He said if it wasn't for me, he could have protected her."

"Right." Hernán said, his voice full of irony. "Protected her black-and-blue."

Claudia wiped her nose with the back of her hand. "Better black-and-blue than bled to death. He was right: it is my fault."

He squeezed her to him. "No, darling. No. It was the murderer who killed her. Not you. Not you." He lifted her chin and looked into her dark eyes, red rimmed from her tears. "Are you all right? He didn't . . ." He couldn't say the words.

She shook her head. "No. Not that."

"How did you get away from him?"

"I apologized. I mollified him. I told him I was wrong. I gave him all the money in my purse. Oh, Hernán, I did not know what I was doing. I started to tell him my whole life story. About my grandmother, the war widow from Paraguay. About my mother dying when I was only eight. I kept thinking in the back of my mind how Luz was like me, raised by her grandmother and her father, and how very different my childhood was, living with kind people who adored me."

She was overcome with grief. He went to the kitchen and brought her a glass of water.

She took a sip and kissed his hand. "When I realized Torres was falling asleep, I just kept talking and talking until the knife fell from his hand and then I snuck out of the door and crept up the stairs to home."

He slumped onto the sofa beside her. "Where I treated you like shit."

She raised her eyebrows and smiled. "That is a rude but accurate description of how you behaved."

BLOOD TANGO • 159

"Why didn't you stop me? Why didn't you tell me the whole story?"

"My father was still here. After he left, you started to get angry and . . ."

He pushed her hair away from her wet and exhausted face. "I was sure you were dead," he said. And then he kissed her with all the passion his body had feared it would never feel again.

It was after seven before they disentangled from each other. He felt as if he had repossessed her, taken her back from the brink where she had been. "I was afraid your father would die from grief and I would go crazy without you," he said. "You are the glue that holds me together." He kissed the top of her head as it rested on his shoulder.

The telephone clanged just as the last words left his mouth.

He ran for it, thinking it might be her father, still worried about her. His editor didn't give him a chance to complain about the hour. "The sugar workers in Tucumán have called a general strike in support of Perón. I need you to cover the unions. They are going to hold a big parley today to decide what they are going to do."

"Right," was all he said into the phone. He apologized to Claudia for having to leave her alone today.

"Don't worry," she said. All she wanted to do was hide under the covers all day.

"Swear to me you will call the detective as soon as it's light."

"Oh, I will. Don't worry. I am more convinced than ever that Torres killed Luz."

He kissed her. "And promise that you will stay here. You will not leave this apartment until Torres is in custody. You will open the door to no one but your father or me."

She swore it.

Hernán shaved and took a quick bath. By the time he went back to the bedroom, Claudia was fast asleep. He drew the drapes to darken the room. He would call the detective himself. He stopped by her father's apartment on the way out. "She will probably sleep until noon. You have your keys to our place, right?"

Gregorio nodded.

Hernán did not want to tell the old man the truth. "Make sure she stays home today. Strikes are beginning around the country. The streets could get even uglier than they have been, and if the army decides to march on the city, there will be insanity in the plazas."

"I will sit on her, if I have to," the old man said.

Hernán leaned over and kissed him on both cheeks. "Thank you," he said.

"She is everything to me," Gregorio said.

"To me, too."

What with the darkened room and the depth of Claudia's fatigue, Hernán turned out to be right about how long she slept. It was her father's little dog, whining to go out, that awakened her. She pulled on a robe and found Gregorio and the Schnauzer in her living room. The dog was sitting by the apartment door like a sphinx.

Claudia kissed her father's forehead. "I am sorry I made you worry last evening," she said. She offered no explanation. He must never know what really happened, and she could never lie to him. Not convincingly. He would spot it in a second.

He raised one eyebrow at the vagueness of her apology, but he did not press her for more information. This is how they had managed since her teenage years. It was an unspoken pact based on love and respect. He did not pry, and she did her best not to make him want to. He took her hand and kissed it. *"Querida,"* was all he said.

"I'll get dressed, while you walk Fritz," she said. "Then, I'll make us a coffee." He put on his jacket and his old straw boater and went out with the dog.

Claudia took the detective's card out of her purse and dialed his number, only to find that he was not at his desk. She left a message with the gruff-voiced man who answered Leary's phone.

By the time she had washed and thrown on a pair of slacks and a shirt, her father returned and switched on the radio. "I don't know why I bother," he said. "All they talk about on this thing is what might happen." He took a newspaper from under his arm and handed it to her. "It's the same with this. They don't really know. It's silly, a bunch of grown men behind typewriters and in front of microphones playing guessing games. As if that will stop the rest of us worrying."

Claudia took the paper but laid it aside. "You know, the reporters are afraid to write the truth. The men on the radio are probably even more afraid of speaking it."

Her father followed her into the kitchen. "I guess I slept through breakfast," she said. "Let's have lunch. Outside the kitchen window, clouds skimmed across the sky, intermittently obscuring the sunlight, brightening and darkening the room by turns.

He cranked the coffee grinder while she put water in the espresso pot. "You're not going to the store today?" he asked. It was something between a statement and a question.

"No," she said, "and I wouldn't have any customers if I did. I think I am about to lose my best one." She spooned the grounds into the pot and screwed it together. "Hernán says Perón will leave the country if he can. Evita will go with him, I am sure, and that will be the end of my making clothes for her."

"Your dresses were too good for her anyway," he said. "She is certainly not as elegant as you make her look."

She took a match from a metal box on the shelf and lit the gas under the coffeepot. "My best customers are always like her—women who used to be very poor. Old-money people generally care little for the latest fashions. Evita needs to be a la mode to convince herself that she has arrived."

Her father chuckled. "Yes, and she spoils the effect by

wearing too much jewelry and those awful hats. And she claims she loves that molester of little girls."

"Except that he raised the salaries of the poorest workers, I dislike him as much as anyone. But I cannot dislike Evita. She drew my sympathies the first time she stepped into my shop and pretended she was not intimidated by the prices. I cannot even tell you why she moves me. She can be a viper, but you want to believe what she says because she says it. I cannot help it. I care about her." It was always this way when discussing Evita. No one was neutral on the subject of Evita.

Once she had poured the coffee, her father sat at the kitchen table while she rummaged in the refrigerator. "When I was returning with Fritzy," he said, " I heard angry voices coming from the alley beside the building. It was that disgusting gardener arguing with someone."

At his words, fear prickled Claudia's skin. "Stay here," she said as calmly as she could. She handed him a tin of beef broth and a can opener. "Open this and dump it into a saucepan. I just remembered, I have to make a call."

She went into the living room and dialed Leary's number again. A different man answered. As quietly as she could, to hide her fear from her father in the next room, she told the policeman that it was urgent that they send a car to her address. "There's a lot going on in the city, lady," the policeman said. "We'll do our best."

She put down the receiver gently and kept her curse to herself. She went back to the kitchen. Her father, the unopened can and the opener still in his hands, was looking out the kitchen window. It was lined with glass shelves that held old red, green, and blue bottles that she had collected since she was a little girl. The intermittent light coming through them showed colors on his skin as if he were standing behind stained glass.

"They are shouting now," he said. Even with the window closed, they heard threats and epithets coming from the alley below. He turned away from the window and got to work on the soup can.

"Somebody will report the fracas," she said as lightly as possible. "I was thinking that since there aren't any customers at the shop and I am staying home, you might help me take down the winter drapes and put away the winter clothes."

Her father nodded gravely. After another glance at the window, he made sure her apartment door was locked.

Jorge Webber drove Evita in Domingo Mercante's Chevy past the majestic facade of the Palacio del Agua toward Pierina Dealessi's apartment. He wished he still had the Packard so he could drive her in the elegance she deserved instead of in this nondescript rattletrap. After their trip through the barrios yesterday, she had taken to sitting in the front seat beside him.

He was sure they had not done enough yet to help Perón. She had not entreated the workers with speeches as he had hoped she would. If she had tried, she could have drawn a crowd wherever they went. How could merely chatting with workingmen and their families—one by one, or a few at a time—do the trick? She did not even instruct them in exactly what to do. The boys in the plazas had gotten angry, but she had kept her voice gentle—never acting the firebrand he knew she could be when her ire was aroused. He was afraid they would not rise up unless she told them to.

"Let's not go back to Pierina's," she said. She had Perón's letter in her hand, and she was chewing on the cuticle of her left thumb. "I want to go to see Bramuglia again. He has to help me get a writ."

Webber made a left at the next corner and skirted the monumental statue of San Martín at the edge of the park near the military club to cross toward Bramuglia's office. Before they reached the broad *avenida,* they found themselves in the middle of an unruly anti-Perón rally. Now, Webber was glad they didn't have the easily recognizable Packard. The crowd blocking the street forced him to slow practically to a halt. Suddenly, a man recognized Evita and started to shout, "It's her. It's her."

"Get down," Webber said, and reached out and pushed her down with his hand on her back. She slammed forward so hard that she doubled over. She threw her arms over her head. He held her down and drove slowly, trying to get through the throng in the street, steering with his left hand and practically nudging the people out of the way with the bumpers and the fenders. Fists started beating on the windows and the doors, which fortunately he had thought to lock when they got in. She started to lift her head. He pushed on her back. "Stay down," he said. He leaned on the horn and managed to get to the end of the block and then sped away as fast as the car would take them through the now-deserted street.

"I think we have to get you indoors," he said when they were safely away. "I don't think now is the time to go to Bramuglia's office."

When she sat up, her nose was bleeding.

"Oh, my lady! I am so sorry." Blood was dripping onto the bodice of her pretty, pale-pink dress. He stopped the car. "I am so sorry."

"I need a handkerchief," she said. Her normally pale skin was white as milk.

He took a fresh handkerchief out of his breast pocket and gave it to her. "Put your head back."

She rested her head against the back of the seat. He watched the street to make sure that no one approached.

"Take me to Pierina's," she said when the bleeding had stopped. "I will take this as a sign that I should forget about the writ.

"I won't go out again today," she told him when they reached Dealessi's building, and the doorman opened the car to let her out. Webber was relieved. How could he do his duty and protect her if she went out into the dangers of Buenos Aires on a day like this?

———

Roberto Leary returned to his desk just after noon, leaving his car in the police parking lot, where, among the dowdy black and gray sedans, it resembled a real diamond in a box of dross. The exterior of the police headquarters looked like any other of Buenos Aires's graceful nineteenth-century buildings, but the interior, when Leary entered it, smelled like a jail and a morgue—of shit and decay. He had never gotten used to the odor and after all these years he knew he never would. Since the early-morning call from Hernán, the dressmaker's boyfriend, he had been out looking for Torres. The gardener had not reported to work at 8:00 A.M. and there had been no sign of him at his address or in his neighborhood gin mills, where evidently he often spent most of his time off.

Ireno Estrada and his dummy partner Franco had had no luck picking up the bastard. Now that Leary could charge him with assaulting the dressmaker, he had to get him in custody before he did something worse. He sent the men back out to scour around for Torres and walked back to his desk, spending more time fantasizing about the girl Pilar than about how to catch Luz's killer—whoever he was. Between love and death, he knew which one he preferred. He made a halfhearted attempt to fill out a report, but after a quarter of an hour he discovered he had put the carbon paper in backward. He was cursing the fact that reports were required in triplicate when Estrada and Franco came in at a run. They should have been out looking for the gardener.

"I told you not to come back without Torres. Why are you still here?" he demanded.

"Get back out to your car," Estrada said. "They found a dead body at the apartment of that woman who owns the dress shop." Estrada didn't have to say which dress shop.

Leary trotted behind them down the wide hallway and out to the parking lot. Their patrol car was pulled up behind his Pontiac. They had left the blue light on the roof spinning. Leary tailed them at breakneck speed, with their siren blaring, past the obelisk and into the grid of streets between Córdoba and Santa Fe. The unstable weather seemed to have passed and knots of demonstrators blocked the *avenidas,* as they had for the past few days. The sun glinted off the chrome on his hood as he turned the last corner and pulled up behind Estrada and Franco, who were already out of their car and running.

They slid to a halt on their leather soles behind a small knot of curiosity seekers standing near a raised flower bed at the front of the building. The dressmaker's father—Gregorio Robles—and another man almost as old stood with their feet in the pansies, looking down at a corpse that was partially obscured by the plants. Leary looked around for Señora Robles, but she wasn't there. He mounted the low cement wall that created the bed and stepped over the wrought-iron fence that topped it. He gestured to the people standing along the walk. "Talk to these people and find out what they saw," he told the patrolmen.

He took off his hat as he approached the corpse.

"It's Miguel Garmendia," the old man, Gregorio, said.

"You knew him?" Leary asked.

"Claudia did. The neighbors came up to tell us there was a body. She came down with me and identified him. I sent her upstairs. To keep her safe."

"Good idea." Leary looked closely at the body. Garmendia was lying on his back. Blood from the wound soaked his shirt but not the ground around him. His heart had stopped before he bled to death—unlike his poor daughter. "Who found the body?"

Gregorio introduced Leary to Raul Llorca, the manager of the building.

"Did you see anyone at the scene when you got here?" Leary asked him.

The tall, skinny building manager had a self-satisfied look about him that one would expect to see on emperor. He turned down the corners of his mouth and shook his bald head. "I went to the café across the square to have a coffee. When I got back, I found the body. No one else was around."

"Did anyone touch the body?"

Llorca shook his head again.

"I felt for a pulse," Gregorio said.

Leary lifted Garmendia's shirt. He had been stabbed once in the chest, up into the heart, it looked like. He sent Franco to call for an ambulance to take the body to the morgue in the basement of the central police station. The docs there would figure out how the knife wound had killed him.

Gregorio Robles whispered to Leary that he should go up

and talk to Claudia, something Leary had intended anyway. Once he was satisfied that Estrada had the neighbors under control, he followed the old man into the elevator and up to the third floor.

The *modista* was on edge. No wonder, after having been held captive the evening before.

Her father sat beside her on the sofa and took her hand the way he must have when she was four years old. He proceeded to tell Leary how, an hour or so ago, he had heard Torres in the alley beside the building having a nasty argument with someone, presumably Garmendia. "The men were accusing each other of killing Luz," the old man said.

Claudia pulled her hand out of her father's. "You didn't tell me that he was arguing with Garmendia." Her voice was two octaves higher than usual.

"I didn't want to worry you."

"So you saw Garmendia with Torres?" Leary asked the old man.

"My father didn't know Garmendia," Claudia said. "I was the one who identified him."

"I heard them arguing," Gregorio said. "I didn't see either of them. I recognized Torres's voice. I thought it might be Garmendia, considering what they were fighting about. After they found Garmendia dead, I saw that I was right."

"I guess this means Torres is your man," the dressmaker said.

Leary did not bother to tell Robles that he was making an assumption about who was doing the arguing. He would have liked to believe, as Claudia Robles and her father did, that this proved that either Torres had killed the girl and then killed her father or that Garmendia had killed his daughter, and then Torres had gone after him for it. As far as Leary was concerned, though, this latest development only complicated matters without allowing any clear conclusions.

Maybe Claudia and her father were right. If so, the story would be over as soon as they arrested Torres. He wanted that to be true.

At ten that evening, Pilar drained the last sip of beer from her glass, set it on the bar, and turned back toward the dance floor. She had stopped looking for Leary at the club after days of longing to dance with him again. He was all business, investigating the case, taking Luz's murder more seriously than Pilar had imagined anyone would. But he had never come back to dance, and she had given up on his coming to be with her at the Gardel.

She danced with Mariano when the numbers did not call for him to sing. He was a precise and skillful dancer, but he put all his passion into his singing and seemed to have little left for dancing. In between dances with him, she stood on the edge of the floor and wished for something that would satisfy her body and her soul.

She took a drag on her cigarette, closed her eyes, and listened to Mariano's rich voice caress the words to "Cuesta Abajo." He sounded like thick hot chocolate. If only the promise of that warmth were actually in the man himself, she might like him the way that he wanted her to, but when he came down from the bandstand, took her hand, and led her onto the floor for the next song, no flame kindled between them, and she knew none ever would. He was taller than Leary, handsomer really in a dark, slick-haired way that all her girlfriends admired. His clothes were much more stylish than Leary's. The one time she had gotten worked up enough to go home with him, he had taken off his suit and shirt very carefully and by the time he had folded and hung everything up, her impulse had slipped away and no amount of diddling on his part could bring it back. She moved to the music with him and felt empty; his dancing was like his lovemaking, about as sexy as long division. When the song ended, this man who claimed he was crazy about her went to the microphone without a backward glance.

A hand touched her shoulder. She spun around about to upbraid the boy who would take such a liberty. Leary took her in his arms as if he owned her as the band began "Cotorrita de la Suerta." His dancing was swift and sure. He held her close, and it seemed as if they had danced together all their lives. After only a few steps, even their breathing was synchronized.

"I have been waiting for this," he whispered in her ear.

She told him, "Me, too," communicating louder with her movements in his arms than with her voice.

When the band next took up "Amores de Estudiante,"

with its languorous tempo, his movements became slow and supple, and overwhelmed her with desire. Her dress had a deep V in the back. He slipped his hand under it so that the pressure of his lead in the dance was on her bare skin. He held the pauses for a split second longer than the music required, inflaming her the more. He took a step with his right foot between hers, and with his knee put a fleeting pressure on her thigh. His eyes were closed. He smelled of that minty shaving soap she had recalled so often since the last time they danced. With the final bars of the song, he switched his weight to his left foot, but she held hers on her right and leaned her body completely into his. When the music stopped, she turned her head and brushed his lips with hers.

They could not get their hats and coats on fast enough. "I share my room with two other girls," she said.

He embraced her and kissed her on the threshold of the club. He drove her to his apartment in a quaint, little house in San Telmo. She was hardy able to breathe when they got up the stairs and through the door of his apartment, and took off just enough of their clothing to get at each other.

"Now," she said. "Now."

He sat down on a long, low sofa and pulled her to him. Their climax was swift and so thrilling that when it finally ebbed, they looked into each other's faces and laughed out loud.

"Too fast?" he asked.

"Perfect," she said, her heart still pounding.

He finished undoing the buttons she had never gotten around to on the side of her dress. "The next one will be slower," he said as he slipped the frock over her head and draped it over the end of the sofa. He put his fingers inside her bra and caressed her breast. Then he led her into his bedroom.

TUESDAY, OCTOBER 16

At the dawn hour, Pilar awoke in Leary's arms. She had never felt so safe in her life. She ran her fingertips over the hair on his chest, and her forehead felt his cheek move. She lifted her head from his shoulder and saw his smile.

"I want to love you again," he said and started to turn her onto her back.

She kissed him warmly and sat up. "I have to tell you something."

He sat up, too. His look had turned wary. "About?"

"About the night Luz was killed."

He pulled her to him. "This is not about that," he said and kissed her.

She pulled away. "I saw a man, when I was about to leave the shop to go to the club. He was standing across the street, leaning against the entrance of the shoe store opposite. His face was a bit obscured by his hat, but it was light enough to see him well. He was wearing a tan plaid suit."

"Did he say anything to you when you went out?" His voice was fully alert now.

"I didn't go out that way. I didn't like the looks of him, so I went back inside. I used the alley exit, and I warned Luz to do the same."

"She didn't," he said.

"I know." Tears welled up in her eyes.

"Don't cry," he said. He got up and took a handkerchief from the top drawer of his dresser. He dried her tears and kissed her eyelids. "That guy—what did he look like? Tall? Short?"

"Not even your height, I think, and thinner."

"Puglisi," he said. He got up and went to the other room. He looked lovely in the nude. Muscular. Sturdy. She picked up his handkerchief from the bed and wiped her nose with it. It had an *R* embroidered in blue in the corner.

He came back with the newspaper clipping he had shown her when he first came to the club and also a photo of a man in uniform. He handed them to her. "Him? The guy in the center? Or this one? He's a lieutenant in the army, but he was wearing civilian clothes at the rally."

"I don't know really." She pointed to the union man. "How tall is he?"

"Not quite my height. Slender."

"I don't think it was him." She handed back the picture of Puglisi.

He pointed to Ybarra. "This one is taller, thinner. Over six feet."

"I only saw the man from across the street. I don't think he was that tall, but—" She opened her palms and shrugged. "I don't think I would recognize him if he wasn't wearing his uniform." She handed the photos back to him, and he threw them on the dresser beside the bed.

"I think you would have noticed how tall Ybarra is. It must have been Puglisi. He was at that rally. He's a sharp dresser. He admitted to following Luz, and he hates Eva Duarte with a passion. It's too bad. I didn't want it to be him. I like the guy. But come on—why didn't you tell me all this before?"

"I was afraid. I think it's dangerous to give evidence."

Leary had to give her that. Revenge was the middle name of a lot of criminal minds in Buenos Aires, even those belonging to the men who made the laws. "Tell me everything you remember," he said. "I promise you will not get hurt."

She nodded, trusting him with her heart if not yet with her mind. "It felt strange that he was just standing there. Something about him made him seem dangerous. I went back. I told Luz what to do, but I should have known she wouldn't listen. I feel so terrible. I cannot forget it. I left her there with him outside. She wanted to come with me to the club, but I told her not to. I was afraid her father would show up again looking for her. I left her in the shop. I should have stayed with her. Or taken her with me. I could have saved her."

"She could have seen him, too. If she saw him, she could have locked herself in."

"Luz wasn't like that. Men beat her up all her life, her father, that animal Torres, but she didn't go around suspecting that people would hurt her. Half the time her head was in the clouds, and it only got worse once she met Señora Duarte. Once she started making herself up like Evita, she spent more time looking at her own reflection in the store windows than paying attention to what was going on around her." Now, she couldn't stop her tears.

He took her in his arms and held her. "It was not your fault. You did not kill her."

"I should have saved her." She sobbed into his shoulder. His skin was warm and smelled clean and salty, like the river water after the rains.

He stroked her hair and kissed her neck. "I am going to catch the bastard who did that to her. It was not a random killing. The motive was not robbery or a rape. Whoever did it was out to kill a specific person. If he hadn't gotten her then, he would have found another time or place." He lifted Pilar's chin and kissed her damp eyes. "It was not your fault, and I promise you we are going to hang him, whoever he is."

She tried to smile at him, but she was sure it did not look like much.

"Listen to me," he said. "Garmendia is dead, and it seems pretty clear that Torres killed him. I have my guys looking all over for him." He held back that Torres had accosted the *modista* with a knife. Pilar was already terrified. He would have to find a way to protect her without making her fears worse.

He stood up. "I am not going to want to do much of anything but make love to you for a good long time, but I have to get to work. If Torres killed Luz as well as her father, that will be the end of it, as soon as we find the son of a bitch."

He put his fingers over his mouth. "I'm sorry, I should not have used that language in front of you. I'm not used to talking over the details of cases in front of ladies."

Pilar looked down at her naked body and back up at his apologetic eyes and laughed. "I've heard those words before. And worse. And worse is what he should be called."

He sat beside her and took her in his arms. "I am going to pursue the Evita–look-alike idea, too. The guy you described doesn't sound at all like Torres or Garmendia. He could be an innocent bystander, but he could be the murderer. I want you to get a close look at Puglisi in person. It might have been him. He's the one who best fits your description."

She shuddered. "I am still afraid of him. That's why I didn't tell you I saw someone. I was afraid if I put the finger on the murderer, he would kill me, too. He saw me looking at him."

He took her hands in his. They were soft, like the silk she sewed. "Has anyone been following you? Have you had threats?"

"No one following me that I know of. I have been watching. No one has threatened me. I am not sure the guy in the doorway had any idea who I was. I don't remember ever seeing him before that evening. But I am afraid if he finds out who I am—" She did not finish.

"I will protect you." Leary looked into her eyes. "You can trust me. Do you believe me?"

"I knew that when I woke up this morning. That's why I had the courage to tell you."

"Nothing will happen to you. I will arrange for you to see Puglisi, and if he was the guy, he'll be arrested immediately. I will make sure you are not left alone with him. You will not be in danger in any way."

"Will he see me? Will I have to testify against him? Suppose he has friends who will come after me?"

He paused long enough in answering to show her that he had not thought of these things. "I will make sure he does not see you. You will see him, but he will not see you. I will arrange to have you protected when it comes to trial."

She knew he meant it, but she was still afraid. Criminals had their ways. Everyone said the country was on the verge of civil war. Their beautiful city had turned brutal. If it remained in an uproar, why would anyone care what happened to a girl like her—with no family, with nothing to recommend her. "I am illegitimate," she said. There were men who would drop a girl for such an admission. He would have to find out sooner or later. Better now than when she was in deeper, needed him more. Her heart wobbled. It was already too late for her. She was head over heels.

He stood up and put both hands on her shoulders. "Pilar." It was the first time he had spoken her name to her. "I never expected this to happen to me right now. The world is falling apart around us. But what is between us is not going away. There is not a bone, not a tissue, not a drop of blood in my body that doubts that." Then, he took her in his arms and made love to her. Not with the urgency and hunger of the night before, but with a passion and openness that made her feel as if they were stitching their souls together.

When they finally let go of each other, she put on his shirt from the night before and made coffee and some toast while he bathed. She liked his narrow kitchen. It had a Philco electric icebox and a window that overlooked the fire station next door. She wished she would never have to leave.

She sat on his bed and drank coffee and watched him dress. She fingered the blue-and-white-striped linen of the bedding. "These are nice sheets."

His reflection in the mirror smiled at her while he tied his tie. "I didn't pick them, but I like them, too."

He put on his jacket and handed her a key. "Stay here," he said. "Call Señora Robles and tell her that you cannot come in to work."

"There is not that much to do there these days anyway. No one is making appointments for fittings."

"I would imagine not. If the man you saw was Puglisi, or whoever it was, he will not be looking for you here. I will come back as soon as I can set up a way for you to see Puglisi without him seeing you. When we know if he was the loiterer in the doorway, I'll know what to do next."

She kissed him good-bye at the door and then went to

the window and watched him get into his beautiful red American's car and drive away and wished he would always be hers.

On his way to work, Leary pondered the investigation in between intense flashes of desire brought on by images of Pilar sitting on his blue-and-white-striped sheets, wearing only his shirt and talking to him as frankly as if they had been friends from birth.

He rearranged the facts in his mind, trying to get them to fit together, but there were too many unanswered questions. For one, neither Torres nor Garmendia fit the description of the man Pilar had seen outside the shop on the night of the murder. Nor did either of them seem like the type to wear a tan glen plaid suit. Ever, in their entire lives. And two of them, each accusing the other, did not jibe with one of them being guilty.

Then again, the short man in the flashy suit could have been standing at the door of the shoe shop waiting for his brother-in-law to come and drive him home. Who was to say? He would find out more when he arrested Torres.

After checking that Franco, the idiot, had not loused up his simple assignment of getting an ambulance to take Garmendia's body to the morgue and getting it positively identified, Leary went to find Estrada, whose interviews with the *modista*'s neighbors had only confirmed what Leary had already learned. Everyone who had been within earshot confirmed Gregorio Robles's story, that Garmendia and Torres had had a shouting argument yesterday morning and had accused each other of killing Luz.

Leary called and confirmed that Puglisi was at work, so he could be easily found. He tried to retype his spoiled crime report from the day before without getting an erection from having his mind wander to Pilar. Eventually, Franco and Estrada came back from seeking Torres. The gardener had still not returned to his apartment, nor had he shown up in any of the places his neighbors said were his favorite drinking holes. No one had a clue where else he could be.

Leary then tried to round up some extra men to search for him but found not a single soul. With pro- and anti-Perón demonstrations, near riots if the truth be told, breaking out all over Buenos Aires, it seemed unlikely that anyone on the force would spend ten minutes looking for a nobody suspected of killing his ex-girlfriend's drunkard father. He would have to find Torres somehow on his own. In the meantime, he was starving. And missing Pilar.

He called her at his apartment. The strains of "Tanguron" were playing in the background when she answered. "From the sound of the music, you've found my Victrola and tango records."

"Yes," she said, "and your books. You have lovely books. Not much food, though."

"Don't go out," he said. "I will bring you a sandwich. Stay inside."

"Don't worry. I am staying here."

He wanted to tell her he loved her, but it seemed too soon. "I'll be back as quick as I can," he said instead, aware of a stirring below his waist. He had too much to do today. But he knew what he would do after dark. No night shift for him tonight.

He drove to an Italian store not too far from his house and bought bread and cheese and delicious fried rice balls with meat sauce in the center that the Sicilian proprietor sold at lunchtime. He wondered if Pilar would like a beer. He bought two and a bottle of orange soda.

At the club she drank highballs. Not like a drunk. She sipped them. He didn't know anything about her. Except that she had no family. Had she known her father? Where had she learned to sew well enough to have the job she had at her age? How old was she anyway? She wasn't the virgin his grandfather had told him he should marry. He had never wanted a virgin—too much work, too much responsibility. All he knew was that he had to have her. And she seemed to want him as much as he wanted her. He wondered if she would think he was some kind of animal if he tried to make love to her as soon as he got through the door.

He found a parking place on the side of the building, though he preferred to leave the car in front, where he could keep an eye on it. The closer he got to Pilar, the faster he moved. He let himself in the downstairs front door with his key, but he knocked on his own apartment door before he went in.

She called out, "Come in."

He prepared himself to hold back from jumping all over her. The second he saw her, his passion evaporated. She sat on the sofa with her arms crossed and eyes full of suspicion and wrath. She was wearing the dress she had had on the night before, too fancy for the daytime.

"What's the matter?" He could not fathom what could have made her angry between the time he had spoken to her on the phone and now. "I brought you lunch," he said, holding up the brown paper sack from the store. It was all he could think to say, and it softened her not at all.

"I am not hungry," she said coldly.

Her behavior completely stymied him. Women were incomprehensible. "You said on the phone there was no food. You must be hungry. "

"I already told you. I am not." There was not a glimmer left in her of the warmth of last night or the trust of early that morning.

He went into the kitchen and made up a couple of plates and poured the beer into glasses. Girls liked to drink beer out of glasses. Of that he was sure. He put the plates on the little kitchen table, near the window, and carried the beers into the living room.

Now she was crying. He sat next to her and tried to put a hand on her arm. She slapped it away. He lost his temper. "Oh for Christ's sake. What did I do?"

He got no answer but sobbing and then silence. He knew better than to yell again.

"You better take me home," she said.

He stood up. "I am going to eat something first." He went into the kitchen and wolfed down some bread and cheese. And drank the orange soda.

When he went back into the living room she was standing by the door, holding her little purse. That's when he realized that she wanted him to explain something. There was Subte fare in that little bag of hers. If she was really done with him, she would have gone home rather than wait for him to come home so that she could stage this little drama. "What made you think you could not trust me?" he said.

"How do you know something made me not trust you?" She was trying too hard to show him he was wrong. She was so cute. So hurt and soft under all this fake anger.

"I am a detective," he said.

Her mouth twisted. It could be the beginning of more wrath or tears, but neither came.

"What did you do while I was gone?" She could have made phone calls. Certainly she had taken a bath. He could smell his soap on her.

"I looked for a towel," she said, as if that should answer the mystery.

"A towel. Did you find one?"

"Eventually." The sarcasm had returned to her voice. Now he was getting somewhere.

"What else did you find?"

Now the tears started to fall again. "I found your other girls."

"In the closet in the bathroom with the towels?"

He had her now. He knew it all. And she saw that he was going to win this one. She was struggling to stay angry and not cry.

"You have lots of girls," she said. "What do you need with me?" There was real anguish in her voice. His heart fell on the floor.

He took her by the hand and went into the bedroom. He opened the top drawer of his dresser and took out the pictures. "You've been looking at these?"

She nodded. "Even if you are not with them anymore, you keep their pictures. You have had a lot of girls. You will pick me up and drop me, too."

He wanted to laugh out loud. He wanted to tease her by saying he would never drop any of the girls in those pictures, but he couldn't bring himself to prolong her agony.

She stamped her foot and punched him, but it didn't hurt. "Why are you smiling? It's not funny."

"Oh, but it is," he said. He held the pictures at the level of her face. "Señorita Borelli, I would like you to meet my sisters. This is Carmen. She is a year and a half older than me. She's married and has three children. This is Emilia. She is five years younger. She is a nurse at the Hospital for Sick Children and is engaged to a mathematics teacher. And this is Norma. She is eleven years younger and still in *colegio*."

She pointed to another, still in the drawer. "And this one? She is the prettiest of all." She was still defensive.

He put his head back and laughed in pure glee. "I have been thinking about her a lot for the past few hours. I want her to like you. In fact, I want her to love you. When I tell her what you just said, I am sure she will. That's my mother. Also Emilia, the Spanish beauty who stole my Irish father's heart."

More tears dropped. "You want to introduce me to her?" She spoke as if she hardly believed it.

He hardly believed he had said it. He had thought about it while he was driving home just now, but when it occurred to him, it had seemed months in the future. She looked at him as if he had already asked her to family lunch next Sunday. He would not be able to go back on it now and didn't want to anyway. So he kissed her instead.

She threw her arms around him and wept into his shoulder and held him so tight that he could hardly breathe. He looked at his watch. "Wait. Wait," he said, though significant parts of his body did not want to wait. "We have to go in five minutes. I have to get you home to your place to change. If I take you to spy on Puglisi this afternoon in that dress, there is no way you won't be noticed."

Back in her home on the Calle Posadas, Evita did not eat the lunch Cristina tried to serve her. Miguel Angel Mazza had called her at Pierina's to tell her that he had to speak to her in private. Since she could not ensure privacy at Pierina's and she was still wary about traveling around the city, she had asked the chauffeur to take her home.

She barely had time to refuse the offered food when the

courtly Mazza arrived. Evita asked Cristina for coffees and went with him into the salon.

"I have given up on Bramuglia," she told him. "I don't know what to do next." She did not mention her Sunday drive through the *villas miserias*. She was still unsure of what he and Perón's other supporters would think of her actions. "I don't want to give up trying to get Perón released, but it seems impossible. I have packed our bags to leave. I don't know what else to do."

Mazza smiled at her, like an indulgent father. The kind of father she had had, but who had abandoned her and her brother and sisters. "Don't worry. As long as we do what we can, but very quietly, it will be the right thing."

She nodded. She believed these words as if they came directly from Perón's lips. She burned to shout, but she took Mazza's words into her heart. She had to find a way to work, but quietly.

Mazza put a hand on her shoulder. "I wanted to see you privately," he said, "because I have excellent news, but we must not let anyone know about it. I think we have found a way to get Perón back to Buenos Aires."

Her heart leaped. "Out of jail. Without a writ?"

Mazza motioned with his hand as if to slow her down. "Not free. But as a first step, we can get him out of Martín García."

She could not understand exactly what he meant but it made her afraid. He must have seen that in her face because he whispered, "By faking an illness."

She felt wary, as if Mazza were trying to break it to her easy that her colonel really was ill. "What good would that do?"

"We will bring him to the military hospital here in Buenos Aires. He will be nearby when Step Two takes place."

"Step Two?"

"Events are afoot," he said. "There may be a way to bring the Fárrell–Avalos government down and put Perón back in power, but on top this time."

While Leary sat on Pilar's little cot and watched her, she changed into a plaid pleated skirt and plain white blouse, trying to make herself as nondescript as possible.

"Do you have something that will cover your hair?"

"My hair?"

"It's very beautiful," he said. "A man would remember it. I am going to try to fix things so that Puglisi doesn't see you, but I want to make sure, even if he catches sight of you, that he won't recognize you."

She dug into a beat-up old trunk at the foot of her narrow bed and found an old straw cloche that had belonged to her mother. She pulled it on and looked in the mirror. It covered all but a small fringe of her hair.

"Good," Leary said. "Let's go. I told him I would meet him at the union hall at three. We'll be lucky if we make it in time."

She felt guilty that she had delayed him with her jealousy, but happy, so happy that her joy sent her fears away.

"Here's my plan," Leary said. "There's a dingy coffee bar near his office. I am going to get him to go there with me. You will already be there. There are a couple of tables in the place, one away from the window where there is not much light. You will sit there and pretend to read the newspaper. I will come in and stand at the bar and have a coffee with him. I will try to get him in a position where you can get a good look at him without him taking notice of you. Then I will go back to the hall with him. Once he and I leave, you will immediately go to my car. I will leave the key with you. You get in the car and lock yourself in. I will break off my conversation with him as soon as I can and meet you at the car. I'll take you to police headquarters, where you can swear out an affidavit. Then I'll get a warrant for his arrest. He will be in custody by six o'clock."

She found it thrilling to be helping him catch a criminal, but she was still afraid. "Suppose I am not sure?"

He looked disappointed. "You will tell me the truth?"

"Yes."

"As long as you tell me the truth, it will be okay."

"Suppose it isn't him?"

He looked even more dismayed. "Then I will take you home."

"Home?"

"To my house. Or to yours. Whichever you want."

She wanted it to be his. She didn't want to disappoint him. She almost hoped that the murderer would be Puglisi, so that Leary would be proud of her for helping him catch the killer. But she was too afraid to hope too hard.

Leary parked the car three blocks from the union hall, bought a newspaper at the kiosk in the corner of the square, and waited around the corner while Pilar took the paper into the café. He gave her time to order a coffee. She was counting out her change to pay when he went past and on to the union hall down the block.

As he entered the dim, smoky office, someone was saying, "All the workers support Perón."

"Think about it, Tulio," another voice shouted. "Without him you wouldn't have a paid vacation. Nobody loves going to the beach more than you."

Tulio answered with his typical refrain, "Yeah. Hitler gave me health insurance. Mussolini gave me a week at the seashore in Mar de la Plata. Hooray! Let's have a party!"

The same voice that had spoken before said, "Watch out, Tulio—if you keep mouthing off like that, they will label you a communist and ship you off to the camps in Patagonia and no one will ever hear of you again."

Evidently, his fellow union leaders were just as bored with Tulio's rants as Leary was, because they all walked away from further discussion. Leary suggested a break, and Tulio's eyes lit up immediately. He grabbed his jacket to go out to the café.

When they went in, Leary took off his fedora and put it on a hook next to the door. As he had hoped, Puglisi did the same with his hat, giving Pilar a clear view of his face. She was sitting, her back to the corner, with a newspaper open on the table in front of her. She was chewing on her forefinger and giving a good imitation of reading the movie schedule. With her head down and her hair covered, and in that dowdy outfit, Leary would not have recognized her himself had he not already known it was she. Carefully, he placed himself between her and Puglisi, giving Pilar a good view of Puglisi's face.

"They are going to strike on the eighteenth," Puglisi said. He held up two fingers and pretended to drink from a demitasse cup—the hand signal to the barista for a double espresso. Leary raised a thumb to order the same.

"I already know about the strike," Leary said. "The cops are always warned." He knew Puglisi would get suspicious if he pretended to be there for chitchat about the political chaos. "I wanted to ask you again about what happened after Perón's farewell rally."

Puglisi stared daggers at him. "Are you still on that nonsense? The country's falling apart, man."

"Yeah, I know. I'm a flunky," he said. "There is absolutely nothing I can do about the insanity in this town, so I am amusing myself with this little murder. It passes the time."

The barista put down two cups. Pretending he was maneuvering for the sugar, Leary managed to change places, so that Puglisi was no longer facing Pilar.

While Tulio was downing his coffee, Leary glanced at her. She shook her head, stood up, and left. As she passed them on the way out, she kept her head down and her face obscured. She was smart, this one.

"Look," Puglisi was saying, "I told you last time. I don't know anything more about this. Don't you have anything to do but to hound me for information I don't have? As far as I am concerned, you should be arresting Perón's actress before she stirs up even more trouble. There must be some law on the books that you could use. Not that the lack of legal backup has ever stopped the present government from tossing anyone it wants into jail."

"Okay," Leary said. He drank the last sugary drop of the coffee. "I had to be sure." Puglisi was right about who got arrested and who didn't. Some people were allowed to protest the government and some were not. The generals had their reasons for who got picked up. Someone might understand the reasons, but they were never made clear to the arresting officers.

"And are you going to leave me the fuck alone about this now?" Tulio was loud and incredulous. The barista looked a bit scared.

"Keep your temper, for Christ's sake," Leary said. "It's one thing to be passionate about politics, but it doesn't pay to come across as someone on the verge of violence."

Puglisi threw a handful of coins onto the bar and started for the door. "You sound like my mother," he said over his shoulder.

They grabbed their hats. Leary jammed his on his head. "I'd listen to my mother if I were you."

"Fuck you," Puglisi said under his breath as they parted company.

Leary rushed to the car. Pilar was sitting in the passenger's seat, wearing that ugly hat and an expression to match. She looked so angry that he was surprised she unlocked the door for him. *Here we go again,* he thought.

"Are you sure it wasn't him?" he said. He reached for the ignition, but the key was not in the dash.

She held it up, dangling from the rabbit's foot key chain that had brought his uncle luck in New Jersey. Evidently, the charm had lost its potency when it crossed the equator to Argentina—at least as far as women were concerned. He took the key, turned the car on, and started the motor. "So?" he said.

"So?"

He shook his head. "So, what have I done wrong now?" Maybe he wouldn't introduce her to his mother after all.

"You told that Tulio guy you're amusing yourself. 'It passes the time,' you said." She did a creditable imitation of his voice. "That's what I am to you. A pastime."

He jammed his foot on the clutch as if he wanted to kill it, as if a new clutch for this car would be an easy thing to come by in Buenos Aires. He could not suppress a groan of exasperation. "I was lying to him. I had to lie to cover up what we were doing."

"Lying? You do a lot of that, it seems. Is that why you slept with me? To get me to spy for you?"

"Is that what it seemed like to you?" He backed up until

he was in position to pull out of the parking space, put the car in gear, and popped the clutch so that the tires squealed, as if new ones for this car would be easy to find as well.

He couldn't say more without shouting, so he shut up. He drove her to her house.

"So I guess that's it. You got what you wanted from me." She pressed the chrome handle to get out of the car.

He grabbed her by the wrist harder than he had intended to. "Wait."

She tried to wriggle free. "Let me go. You got the answer to your question about your 'little' murder. You've taken me home. You're done with me, so let me go." She twisted again to get free.

Part of him wanted to comply, but another part, about halfway between his gonads and his heart, would not let him. "Please," he said, "you are so smart about so many things, I thought you would understand. I was lying to a suspect. Cops do that all the time. I have not lied to you. I swear I haven't."

She let her arm go limp. There was pain in her face but a tiny glimmer of hope in her eyes.

"Please," he said, "get some things—clothes, whatever you are going to need, so we can go home."

She looked him in the eye. He had no idea what she was thinking. "Wait for me here," she said. "I'll just be a minute." She did not smile.

He hoped he could trust her to come back. If she were one of his sisters, she could take hours deciding which shoes to pack. He wanted to talk to her more about Puglisi, find out how sure she was that Tulio was not the man she had seen the night Luz died. But he knew better than to bring that up before he had made love to her again. If she came back.

That afternoon, some minor worker demonstrations broke out in plazas around the city: along the Avenida 9 de Julio, in the Plaza de los Congressos, and in front of the old Cabildo, the Colonial seat of government across the Plaza de Mayo from the Casa Rosada. Prowling on the outskirts of a group circling the enormous equestrian statue of San Martín in the plaza named for him, Evita met a young man, sitting on a stone bench, who, like her, was observing the unionists as they called for "Perón, Perón!" The young man had an analytical look in his intense dark eyes as he took in the scene. Evita approached him, and he looked quizzically at her, as if he was afraid to show that he recognized her. She sat next to him, smiled, and said, "Hello. My name is Eva Duarte."

He said her name in unison with her. They laughed. "I know your face," he said. "My girlfriend reads *Guinón*, the movie magazine. It sometimes has your picture on the cover." He extended his hand to her. "My name is Juan Jiménez."

She felt a bit wary. "Are you a student?" The vast majority of students despised Perón.

"No, I am twenty-three; I'm a teacher."

She gestured toward the workers, many of them in shirtsleeves. She and Perón called them *descamisados,* but they were not really shirtless. Hatless, jacketless, some of them, but not really shirtless. "What do you think of all this?"

"I think that the teachers need a union," he said earnestly. "We are badly paid. We get no pensions and no respect from anyone in the government, hardly from our own students."

She gestured to the demonstrators again. "If these laborers don't get what they are chanting for, there will be no hope for the unions that already exist. I can't imagine the army or the oligarchy favoring a new one for teachers."

He nodded. "I think you are right." He looked longingly at the young men circling the plaza, as if he wanted brothers.

Evita looked over her shoulder. Jorge Webber had parked the car at the bottom of a flight of stone steps that led from the park to the street below. He was leaning against it and reading the newspaper. She turned to Juan Jiménez. Juan was an important name for her. Her father, her brother, Perón—all were named Juan. Her mother was Juana. "Juan," she said, using the familiar address, "help me get them what they want, what we all need." Perón had said it: the day they arrested him at Tres Bocas, that if the *descamisados* rose up to support him, nothing could stop them. She saw a way, a very quiet way, to get them to do that.

"How can I help?" Jiménez's voice was confused but energized.

"Just wait here a moment."

She went down the stairs to Jorge. "Please," she said, "I need you to go to the *modista* and pick up a suit I asked her to make for me."

He looked at her, incredulous. "A new dress? Now?"

She felt like slapping him. "This is important, whether you think so or not. Tomorrow or the next day or the day after that will be the most important day of my life. I have to look the part when the time comes. If I am going to achieve my goal, I must do something very important right now. And I need you to do what I asked. Is that clear?"

He folded his newspaper and got into the car.

She went back to Juan Jiménez on the bench. "We have to tell them," she said. "Each of them needs to bring their brothers tomorrow."

She moved toward the men circling the grand monument to the liberator of Argentina. She could not make speeches to the union leaders, especially knowing that so many of them thought her a *puta* because she lived with a man who was not her husband. But now she had found her way. And this young man could help her. He stood up and followed her. She rubbed her sweaty palms on her skirt and held a hand out as she approached one worker, just one, who looked at her expectantly as she walked toward him. He took her hand very briefly and gently. "Listen," she said, speaking to the one man, alone. "Tomorrow, you must come back, and you must bring ten others with you, and tell them to bring ten people. Everyone needs to tell ten people to bring ten people. And if that doesn't force them to free Perón, the next day everyone needs to bring ten more people who will tell another ten people to bring ten people."

Jiménez watched her urge a couple of others, and soon he

was also speaking to the men, one to one. And soon they were gathering around him and around her and listening and talking to one another. There was no shouting. No more chants of "Perón. Perón." Just talking, almost whispering the message. *Tell ten more. Tell them to bring ten more.*

When she came out of her tiny apartment, Pilar looked into Leary's sexy red car and saw him asleep. She carried her little cardboard suitcase with her favorite clothing, the things she had made herself with remnants Señora Claudia had let her take. She opened the door with trepidation. He woke up instantly and grinned at her. "That didn't take long."

She put her head inside the car. "I'm sorry I was cranky," she said. "I am not used to—"

He reached out and put his fingers gently on her lips. "Let's just go home," he said.

She flashed him that irresistible smile and put her valise in the backseat and closed the door.

He started the car. "My sister Emilia would have taken until nightfall to pack her clothes." He shifted the Pontiac into Reverse.

"I don't have that much to choose from." She knew he would be angry when she told him where she needed to go. She bit her lip and spit it out: "I got a call from Señora Claudia. I have to go to the shop. She has a job for me to do."

"What? Oh, come on. Who is buying dresses on a day like today?"

"It was an order the customer gave us two weeks ago. We promised it for tomorrow. The lady is going to a baptism over the weekend in Montevideo. She's coming in for a fitting, and I will have to make some adjustments."

Baptism, my ass, Leary thought. He figured the customer was Eva Duarte. "My guess is that the lady in question is leaving the country for more than just the weekend."

"I have to go," she said. "I can't lose my job. We have so little work these days. We have to cater to the customers we still have left."

He drove directly to the shop. As a policeman he could drive on Florida, though the street was closed to traffic during store hours. Not that it mattered today, when no one was shopping except for that dame going to a "baptism," who would probably stay away for the rest of her life. Which might be a good thing all around. When Leary had first gotten involved with this investigation he had not thought deeply about the political implications of what was going on in Argentina. He hated being part of the Federals because they were more like part of the army, keeping the fat cats in power. And it turned his stomach that he might be assigned to arrest people whose only crime was not agreeing with the generals. But he had always heard from the men on the force that Perón was good to the workingman. He had thought of the colonel as more or less a good guy. But now he was not so sure. In fact, not sure at all.

When he pulled up in front of the shop, he took her hand. "While you are here I am going to headquarters. Tell me again. You are absolutely sure the guy you saw outside the shop that night was not Puglisi?"

"Positive." She had her other hand on the door handle. Her eyes were clouded with fear.

He had still not found the bastard who'd killed Luz. He had promised to keep Pilar safe. He was desperate to keep her safe. He slipped across the seat toward her and put his arm around her waist and kissed her with all his heart. "Stay here," he said. "When you are ready to leave, do not leave the shop. Wait here. I will pick you up. Okay? You must not go out alone."

She put both arms around his neck and kissed him hungrily. She took his breath away.

"Promise me, you will do as I said."

"Yes," she said and held him close for a minute, her face buried against his chest.

A faint tinkling of a bell sounded behind her as a man in a chauffeur's uniform—gray jacket with pewter buttons, matching jodhpurs, and tall black boots—came out of the shop, carrying a woman's suit on a hanger. As he put on his black peaked cap, he glanced in at them and then turned and walked away toward the corner of Córdoba. He looked familiar.

Pilar still had her arms around Leary and tried to kiss him again. "What is it?" she asked. Her eyes searched his.

He couldn't remember where he had seen that man. He

was dressed like twenty or thirty other drivers in the city. "Nothing." He kissed her. "Go in. But don't come out unless you are with me. Promise?"

"I already promised. I won't."

She gave him her full sunny smile, the one he'd seen when he told her he wanted to introduce her to his mother. There were words for how that smile made him feel, but he didn't tell them to her. Not yet. He kissed her one more time and watched her cross the sidewalk and go into the shop. She was beautiful from the back.

Then he drove to the end of the block to see if he could find the chauffeur with the lady's suit. The street was deserted except for an ordinary gray Chevrolet sedan pulling away, not the kind of car that came with a uniformed driver. Leary wanted to follow it, just in case, but this was where his car was a liability. You could never use one this red, with this much chrome, with big white-walled tires, to follow anyone. A cop needed a nondescript car for that. He squelched his hunch and let the Chevy get away. He had no reason to think anything of the man in the jodhpurs.

Then, on his way back to headquarters, it hit him where he had seen the man. He was Eva Duarte and Juan Perón's chauffeur. On a hunch, Leary drove to their apartment house on Posadas, and when he arrived, he saw the same man carrying the suit into the building. He guessed then that the lady who was going to the baptism was not Evita, after all. Whatever Pilar had gone into the shop to sew, it couldn't be what Perón's chauffeur had already picked up. He was not sure what to make of all this. He let it sit in the back of his mind and went back to the police station.

When he got there, he called the dress shop and made sure that Pilar was still there. He got Claudia Robles on the phone. She, of course, wanted to know whether they had arrested Torres.

Leary wanted to believe Torres was the murderer. And that the flashy man Pilar had seen was not involved. But his niggling doubts would not give up the notion that the murder had something to do with Luz's impersonating Eva Duarte. He made Claudia Robles promise not to let Pilar out of her sight.

He went to find Estrada and Franco. To his amazement, they had Torres in custody. "The owner of a bar near his house told us he roots for the Juniors, and he doesn't have a radio. He always goes to the bar to listen to the games. He bets on them. The Juniors had a big match with Tucumán. Franco and I showed up just as the match was ending. There he was, drunk as a skunk."

"His team lost," Rudolfo Franco added and beamed, so proud that such a thought had come into his pea brain.

Leary patted him on the back. "Keep thinking like that and they'll force you to become a detective, Rudi."

Estrada laughed. "Maybe him, but not me, Robo. I don't want it. Detectives don't get time and a half for overtime." It was a fact Leary knew well.

He went down to the basement of the building, where they held prisoners in cells adjacent to the morgue. One of the tortures the suspects were forced to endure was the nasty smell of formaldehyde in the police headquarters' nether regions.

Leary got the guards to put Torres in an interrogation room and went in to talk to him. No one had questioned him yet, which didn't surprise Leary. Men could be kept in this tomb for months before anyone paid any attention. It was one of the things the people were calling for: the return to constitutional government that would force the cops to behave. Leary had to admit they had a point.

Torres looked like shit and carried its perfume as well. He was big and stocky. There was nothing about him that said "gardener," except that his forearms and face were tanned from working in the sun. It was hard to believe that this thug spent his time pruning rosebushes. Leary did not bother to introduce himself. "Do you know why you are here?" he asked.

"Yeah, I stabbed that bastard Garmendia."

Leary was taken aback. He had never been able to get any suspect to confess to anything. This was too easy. "I see. Why did you kill him?"

Torres coughed for a full minute before he could say anything. The man's breath gave Leary a hard lesson in where the shit smell was coming from. "You got a ciggy?" Torres asked.

"I don't smoke," Leary said.

Torres smirked as if Leary had said, *I'm a sissy.*

"I'll get you one," Leary said. "Tell me first, why did you kill Garmendia?"

Torres blew out another dog breath. "Because he killed Luz, and the son of a bitch had the balls to accuse me of doing it."

"How do you know Garmendia killed her?" Leary asked.

"She told me."

Leary could not hide his surprise. "When did she tell you that?"

Torres coughed for another forty-five seconds. "She said it a million times. From when she was a baby, her bastard father was always telling her, 'I'll kill you if you shit your pants again.' 'I'll kill you if cry.' 'I'll kill you if—' Fuck. He told her he would kill her for blinking when he didn't want her to."

Leary nodded. "I see. But if he was saying that for sixteen years, what makes you think he actually did it this time?"

Torres just sat there and looked at Leary as if he thought him stupid.

Leary left him for a minute and bummed a cigarette and a match from the guard at the door. Once Torres had lit up and taken a couple of deep drags, Leary asked him again, "Why do you think he killed her at this point?"

"Because she ran away from home. He killed her now because he found her. And the son of a bitch would not tell the truth about it, even when I had my knife at this throat. I told him I was going to kill him anyway, so he might as well admit it."

"And he didn't."

"*No!*" Torres shouted. "And he pissed me off so bad I stabbed him for that. He killed her."

None of this sounded right to Leary. "How do I know it wasn't you who killed her? How do I know he didn't come after you because you killed her? When he accused you, you killed him and left him in your petunias."

"Pansies," Torres said indignantly. "I hate fucking petunias."

Leary nearly laughed in his face. "Yes, well, Garmendia came after you. He must have thought you killed his daughter. Otherwise, why would he have come looking for a younger, stronger man? He had to know he was taking his life in his hands by accusing you. Why would he have done that if he had murdered her?"

Torres took one long, last drag on the cigarette before he dropped the tiny butt on the cement floor and ground it out with his gardener's boot. "Well, if he didn't kill her, then who did?"

"You?"

"I killed her fucking father for saying that." Torres jumped out of his chair and went for Leary's throat. Leary smacked him down and called out for the guard, who was in the room in a second. "Take him back to his cell."

Leary went back to his desk to fill out the paperwork charging Torres with the murder of Miguel Garmendia. He stopped short of putting Luz's name on the list of his victims. There was absolutely no reason for anyone to trust Lázaro Torres, but Leary was pretty sure he had not killed Luz. He was an asshole, but he wasn't an actor. An artless jerk like him could never have given such a convincing performance.

Leary was reversing the carbon paper and getting ready to fill out the back of the form when Pilar called to say she was ready to leave the shop.

"I am coming right now. Stay where you are."

"Señora Claudia is staying with me. She said you asked her to."

"I did."

"Don't you trust me?"

Trusting was not his problem, but it was hers, probably for good reason, he thought. He would prove to her she could rely on him. "Just stay in," he said.

"I am making myself a silk nightgown while I wait," she said and giggled.

"You aren't going to need it," he said. The men in the squad room gave him a dirty look when he laughed into the phone. He rolled the form into the typewriter, left it there, and went to get his girl.

WEDNESDAY, OCTOBER 17

Colonel Miguel Angel Mazza had spent the chilly, damp wee hours of Wednesday morning presenting an old chest X-ray to a navy doctor, pretending it had just been taken. "This proves," he argued, "that Perón needs immediate medical attention."

What Mazza and Perón understood very well was that the seventeenth was the day when they had to make their move. The unions pro and not-so-pro Perón had called for a general strike on the eighteenth. If that took place, it would dilute the attention of the populace by calling for all manner of reforms. What Perón and his adherents needed was a manifestation in support of Perón and no one and nothing else. If it was ever to happen, it had to be today.

At last, at 3:00 A.M., the navy doctor received a telex from the Casa Rosada, authorizing him to release Perón to the military hospital in Buenos Aires. The regime, what was left of it, was unwilling to risk Perón becoming a martyr.

Shortly thereafter, an exhausted Miguel Angel Mazza presented the new orders to the commander of the military prison at Martín García and was given permission to move Colonel Juan Perón to the capital.

At six that morning, a ringing phone awakened Evita, who had tossed and turned in the night, thinking of the workers and wondering if they were doing as she and Juan Jiménez had exhorted them to. Anxiety flashed her awake at the first ring.

"Señora," the voice on the line said. "This is Dr. Mazza." He told her that Perón was in the city.

"Thank you. Thank you," she said. Mazza was such a nice man. He always called her señora, not señorita, as so many of Perón's supposed friends did, emphasizing the *ita* to show that they were very well aware that she and her colonel were not married.

She immediately called Jorge Webber's room, which Perón kept for him on the first floor in the rear of the building. With a groggy voice, he answered after several rings. She told him the news. "We must go to the hospital at once."

"I am sorry, but I cannot," he said.

"What? What do you mean you cannot?" She was incredulous. Perón paid the little squirt plenty for his services. "I will not take no for an answer."

"I am so sorry, but I have a very urgent personal matter I must take care of."

"At this hour?"

"It may take all day."

She blew out a breath of exasperation. As far as she knew, Jorge did not have a personal life. "Very well. Drive me to the hospital and leave me there." She hung up before he could give her any other excuses.

She dressed quickly, but took pains with her makeup. By the time Webber rang the bell, she was standing just inside the apartment door, with her hat on and her purse over her arm, waiting for him.

Evita was surprised to see the chauffeur wearing not his uniform but a cheesy brown glen plaid suit she had never seen before. She could not imagine what he was thinking. This was not the compliant man in jodhpurs. She did not know this Jorge.

"I am sorry, señora," he said on the short drive to the hospital in Belgrano. "I wish I could be more useful."

His tone was, as usual, just this side of obsequious, but, very uncharacteristically, he left her at the entrance to the hospital and drove away as if Domingo Mercante's car belonged to him.

Evita watched the red taillights disappear into the gloomy dawn and made a vow to take his job from him before the end of the day.

At the hospital reception she was outraged to find, within minutes of her arrival, that they would not let her in. "Relatives only," the corporal at the desk told her. He looked away when he said it, so she pressed her case.

He went into an office behind him and brought out a lieutenant with a sanctimonious smile. "I am sorry, señorita," he said without a hint of sincere regret. "Regulations forbid admitting visitors to the treatment rooms if they are not relatives." Both men returned to the office and left her standing there alone. Without asking anyone's permission, she picked up the phone and called for a taxi to take her home.

Angry and humiliated as Evita felt at that moment, she would have been heartened by the scenes playing out under gray, heavy skies at the gates of factories on the periphery of the city; down in Avellaneda near the gates of the meatpacking plants, men arriving for their work shift were greeted by fellow workers urging them to strike that day, to follow them to the center of city. Talk spread quickly among these dark-skinned poor from the Pampas, who had come to Buenos Aires in the last ten or fifteen years. These were not the white, skilled workers of the old unions: men with political philosophies and sophisticated agendas. These *descamisados* had only one clear conviction—their champion had been jailed, and they wanted him out.

Word got around. "The big shots and the kids from the universities are marching through the streets asking for what they want. Why not us?" Plans took hold. When the slaughterhouse workers discussed what it was they would demand, there was only one answer. They all agreed. The name of the only government official who had ever cared a fig about the needs of the people who did the dirty work, people that his fellow well-to-do *porteños* had never set eyes on. These men had only one demand: "Perón. Perón."

Some went home to paint that name on torn bedsheets. Others fanned out to nearby plants and factories where their brothers and cousins worked, to bring the word. Others headed straight for the center of Buenos Aires: that beautiful fairyland of parks and opulent buildings that most of them had never seen in their lives.

At seven thirty, Lieutenant Ramón Ybarra reported for duty at the Casa Rosada and found his boss, General Avalos, already on the telephone, discussing the merits of potential members of a new cabinet proposed by incoming Prime Minister Álvarez. Ybarra listened to Avalos's end of the conversation with growing satisfaction. His boss was doing the expected. The army brass were carefully going over the qualifications of people who would never govern Argentina, because by the time they finished their prissy discussions, he and his fellow junior officers would have risen up and taken over.

While Avalos was on the phone, at his desk across the room, Ybarra called the three key men in his plot, Novara, Cieza, and Garín, to make sure they were readying troops to march the moment things got out of hand in the city. Two of them said they were too busy to talk at the moment, but he should be assured that everything was being arranged. Cieza's aide said he was away from his desk. That might have worried Ybarra except that the tank battalion's barracks were far from their commander's office. He dialed Francisco

Rocco. Cisco's voice immediately lowered to a whisper. "The low-level workers from the factories on the outskirts are converging on the center," he said.

"Today?" Ybarra's voice was so loud it caused Avalos, still on the phone across the room, to look up in alarm. Ramón swiveled around and faced the wall behind him. "Are you sure?" he whispered into the receiver. "I heard the big strike was supposed to be tomorrow."

"Well, something is happening today," Rocco said. "The animals are escaping from the zoo." He laughed.

Ybarra was frozen. "This was supposed to happen tomorrow, not today. We aren't ready to mobilize," he whispered in the phone. "What are we going to do about this, Cisco?"

There was silence at the other end of the line.

Ybarra could barely suppress a groan. "The actress is behind this."

"Oh, come on," Rocco said. "You are obsessed with her."

Ybarra glanced over at Avalos, still on his call. "Listen. You have to get the other guys to move today."

"How?" Rocco asked. "I am not sure—"

Ybarra opened his mouth to insist, but General Avalos hung up his phone and called his name. "I have to go," Ybarra told his friend. "I will call you in a few minutes."

He stood and approached the general's desk. "Sir," he said, "Francisco Rocco just told me that there is a mob of workers coming into the city."

"Yes," Avalos said. "President Fárrell just told me."

"Sir, what are we going to do?"

"The Federal Police are handling it for now. We are going to keep a close eye on the situation."

At that moment, the situation in question, to the south of the center, was heating up. More and more workers continued to gather in small groups in their dirty, overcrowded neighborhoods—La Boca, Barracas, Parque Patricios. The employees of the Swift-Armour plant in La Plata showed up for the first shift but never punched their time clocks. They headed, instead, for the bridges over the Riachuelo, leading to the city center. In Berisso, out by the leather-tanning plants, Cipriano Reyes, one of Perón's most faithful union supporters, watched the parade of laborers coming up toward the canal crossing and was stupefied by the swell of numbers. He had been working to get something to happen today, but he had no idea it would be this huge. He encouraged the men to go on to the Plaza de Mayo in front of the Casa Rosada. Then, he found a telephone and called the printers' union to order placards. "What should we put on them?" the printers' union chief asked.

"Perón. Perón."

When for the third day in a row his phone rang before eight in the morning, Hernán Mantell knew before the government did how massive the worker's demonstration was becoming. He got the call from a photographer at the paper who had heard a rumor from the woman who cleaned his sister's house. "I'm at a pay phone at the end of the trolley line," he said. "You have to get yourself out here. It's going to be bigger than the one Perón held last week when he resigned. It is impossible to get on a trolley toward the center. They are all packed."

Hernán ran his hand through his hair, still wet from his bath. "Good God. Do you have your camera?"

"Of course."

"Okay. Meet me at the old bridge down between La Boca and Avellaneda, the one at Virrey Vieytes. It's a straight shot from where I am. I can get there in twenty minutes. It will make a good picture if we can get a packed trolley crossing the big iron bridge."

Hernán sped back into the bathroom, took off the towel he had wrapped around his waist, and dropped it over the edge of the tub. "I have to go," he said to Claudia, who was still at the sink, brushing her teeth. "A huge demonstration of the working guys from the abattoirs is brewing. They are marching into the center." He went into their bedroom.

He was already threading a belt through his trouser loops when she finished washing her face and followed after him. "You'd better stay indoors today," he said.

"Torres is in custody. I can go out safely. At the very least, I'll have to go to the grocers."

"Sure, but do it early." He was tucking his tie under the collar of his shirt. "Then stay in. I doubt they will come this way, but the city is going to be tied in knots, you can be sure of that." With one arm in his jacket sleeve, he gave her a quick kiss and was out the door.

She turned on the radio, but there was not a word about any worker demonstrations. Not that a lack of news was unusual. The last thing the generals would do was advertise a mass uprising of low-level workers. The marchers would most likely head to Plaza de Mayo to make their demands. If they did, they would be only eight or ten blocks from her store at the most. She put down her hairbrush and started to dress. It was easy for Hernán to say she should stay home, but it was really that store that supported them: her, her father, Hernán too, not that she would ever remind him how little a journalist made in these times of suppression. It did not matter to her who paid their rent, but it would matter to both of them if her shop was wrecked and she lost all that sumptuous fabric she had paid for so dearly at wartime prices. Garmendia was dead. Torres was in jail, where she hoped he would rot. Neither of them could hurt her, but the mob in the center could ruin her business for good.

Vivid pictures fell into her head: of smashed windows and bolts of stolen English Tweed and Italian silk being carried away. Stuff no one would be able to buy anytime again soon, given the destruction in Europe. The faster the images of looting poured into her imagination, the faster she dressed. She put her forefinger through her stocking as she pulled it on and had to find another one. While she was rummaging in her drawer, the phone rang again. She ran and grabbed it.

"Señora Claudia?"

It was Pilar. "I was just going to call you," Claudia said. "There is going to be—"

The girl interrupted. "I know. I am not at home anyway."

She swallowed hard. "Señora, I am staying with the policeman. You know, Roberto Leary."

Claudia put her head back and laughed out loud. Fast worker, her little Pilar. "Oh, good. At least you will be safe with him."

"He has gone out already. They have called in all the policemen, even detectives like him. They are raising the drawbridges over the Riachuelo to keep the worker guys from coming into the center from the south."

Claudia's index finger went to her mouth. Hernán had said something about one of those bridges to whoever had called him.

"Listen, Señora," Pilar said. "I have to talk to you about something. I need you to help me answer an important question."

"Pilar, I am on my way to the shop. I want to make sure it does not get looted by the demonstrators. Can you meet me there?"

"Yes," Pilar said. "That's what I was hoping. It's still quiet where I am. I'll take the Subte."

"Me, too. I'll meet you there. Do you have your key?"

"Yes," Pilar said, her voice suddenly glum. Mention of the key reminded them both that Leary had found it next to Luz's body. "I'll be there soon," the girl said, and rang off.

Claudia imagined that Pilar was in love and wanted to talk about Leary and her chances with him. The girl had no living mother. Claudia, who had also been a motherless girl, was so often the woman that motherless girls turned to. She, a childless woman. It must be something about her. She must have somehow sought them out. Her heart sank at the thought of poor little Luz, the motherless girl given aid by the childless woman. Not aid. She had brought the girl into a situation that ended her life. Nothing good had ever happened to that child, except getting to try on Evita's clothes and model them for her idol. Well, at least now something good might be in store for Pilar.

Claudia pinned on her hat, took her purse, and decided not to tell her father she was going out. He would insist that it would not be safe for her to go alone. He would want to go with her. She had to go and defend her business, but she was not going to risk his getting hurt into the bargain.

While Claudia was tiptoeing past her father's apartment door and sneaking out of her building, Angel Mazza was waiting for Evita in the lobby of Perón and Eva's apartment building on the Calle Posadas. When the actress arrived, she threw her arms around his neck. "They would not let me see him," she said too loudly into his right ear before she let him go. "Were you with him? Have you seen him? How ill is he?"

"Oh, my dear," Mazza said in that courtly way of his. "You mustn't worry. As I told you yesterday, we needed a reason to move him into the center, and I said I had diagnosed pleurisy. It was a disease that would make that damp prison island dangerous. But really, we used an old X-ray to give him an excuse. He is fine."

"What do you think is going to happen next? The city is so quiet." She despaired of her attempts to free Perón. She had said too little. The workers had probably ignored all she and that teacher Juan had said the day before. She had just taken a cab home. Between here and the hospital, nothing was happening.

Mazza smiled at her. "Not quiet for long," he said. "While I was at the hospital this morning, Cipriano Reyes called and said that masses of workers are heading for the center."

She leaped and clapped her hands. "It is working. It is working."

"What is working?"

She told him about the ten bringing another ten.

He looked at her with awe.

"We should go out," she said. "We should gather more and more of them. Do you have a car? We must drive out and speak to them. I would have gone, but our driver has disappeared with Domingo Mercante's car."

Mazza raised his elegant surgeon's hands and patted the air in front of him. "No. No. So far, everything is perfect. But the colonel told me very explicitly that we mustn't seem as if we are behind this. Whatever happens next has to look absolutely spontaneous on the part of the workers. He cannot betray the army directly. In the end it has to look as if he had no choice but to take the reins of government, as if events have overwhelmed him and only he can save Argentina."

Evita heard Perón's subtle logic in Mazza's words, her Perón, the wise and canny man who knew how to be invincible. She threw her arms around the old doctor again. "Don't worry," she said. "It is working."

Not even the determined and hopeful Evita could have imagined how well it was working. Roberto Leary, dispatched along with every available member of the city police force to help keep order, arrived at the Old Ferry Bridge in a patrol car with Estrada and Franco. By the time they got there, local-area policemen had raised the drawbridge to stop the influx of workers into the center of the Buenos Aires. Boisterous and joyful men were backed up on the *avenida,* but they were not giving up. Dozens were swimming the Riachuelo. Others laughed and sang while they constructed makeshift rafts to carry the nonswimmers across. The whole effort carried the atmosphere of a fiesta; cheering and whistling greeted every crossing whether by one person or a full raft. So many piled onto one float made of hastily strung-together boards that it half submerged and barely made it to the other bank.

"There's no stopping them," Leary said. From all he had heard in the past week, Perón was nowhere near the hero these innocents thought he was. Perhaps just the opposite. But they were not some angry mob bent on destruction. They looked as if they wanted nothing more than to do what the rest of the population had been doing for two months—to stand in the street and shout for their rights. "If someone drowns, this could all turn ugly," he called to Franco and Estrada. "Tell them to lower the bridge."

"Yes, boss," Franco said, as if Leary were a foreman on the drawbridge brigade.

When the crossing was opened, young men on the roadway and on the banks below, their shiny black hair dripping river water, let out a whoop of joy. A couple of dozen workers converged on a southbound trolley that had been stopped on the outbound track. "Turn it around. Turn it around," they called to the driver, who held out his hands, palms up. Leary knew he couldn't turn it until he got to the turntable at the end of the line.

The men did not pause. They climbed up onto the roof of the car and disconnected the poles from the overhead wires. "Pablo," one of them shouted. They jumped down from the roof of the trolley.

A relative giant came from the back of the crowd and squatted at the front of the car, grasping the undercarriage. About thirty of them heaved and counted and grunted and, to Leary's and everyone else's amazement and delight, they picked up the trolley and turned it. A couple of the boys scrambled back up on top and reconnected the poles to the overhead conductors. They hung the back of the car with a huge white cloth with *"Sindicato"* scrawled on it in black paint, and the packed trolley took off in the direction of the center with scores of men dancing and singing behind it.

The joy that day was all in the streets. Grim faces looked down from balconies on the happy, thickening crowd going by. The rich peered out from behind brocade draperies and quaked with fear.

In the Palacio Paz, the top army officers walked as if on eggs and spoke in whispers. Their only encouraging news came from a police report that the crowd in the Plaza de Mayo was not very large and not at all organized. Things in the city center were glum but peaceful, and the president decided there was no need for alarm.

When Ybarra asked General Avalos outright if he had any plans to bring troops into the center, the minister of war said, "No." In his judgment, he explained, it was unnecessary even to keep them on standby. A livid Ybarra went to his phone and was further angered when it rang before he could make his call. He picked up the receiver.

"Ramón? Ernesto here."

His lily-livered brother was the last person he wanted to talk to today. "Yes, hello. We are quite busy here."

"Yes, I can imagine. The general asked me to come and see you. I am downstairs in the lobby. Please meet me immediately. I need just a few minutes of your time."

Avalos was speaking into his own phone again, but he was looking at Ybarra with a commanding stare. Evidently, he knew exactly who was calling Ybarra at this moment and what he was saying.

"Fine. I'll meet you," Ybarra said and hung up.

At that moment, waiting on the platform for a Subte

train that seemed never to come, Claudia Robles, like Ybarra, was fuming. She paced and listened to her fellow passengers gossip. "I got a phone call from my sister who lives in the Constitución district," a young woman was telling an older man in a camel-hair blazer. "She said that there are workers crossing over the Riachuelo and heading for the center of town."

The man stood with his hands behind his back and shook his head. "This is the end of tranquility," he said, as if Buenos Aires had seen anything approaching peace and quiet in the last several months.

Claudia looked down the track into the tunnel in the direction of the train that would not come. She wondered, with all the tumult, whether the Subte was working at all. Her whole financial future was in danger. She could not wait any longer, and she could not walk all that distance to the store in the shoes that she had on.

After waiting almost an hour, she gave up and went back home. Calls for a taxi yielded nothing but a busy signal. She knew better than to telephone Hernán to see if he would come and give her a lift. He would only get outraged that she wanted to go to the center in the first place.

Meanwhile, just south of the center, in San Telmo, Pilar was having the same problem. She had already given up, gone back to Leary's apartment, and changed into flat shoes. She walked toward the shop through eerily deserted streets. There were a few small groups of workers passing up the avenues every once in a while. A bunch of men were drinking from a fountain in the small park on the corner of Humberto and Defensa, but by the time she got to the Calle Florida, she saw only shuttered storefronts and empty sidewalks. She decided to go in through the front. Ordinarily, she was required to use the back entrance to avoid disturbing the customers, but there were no customers today; that was certain.

It surprised her that Señora Claudia was not there already, but she figured there were no trains from her neighborhood, either. She raised the shutters and left them up. The señora would be arriving at any moment.

Pilar unlocked the front door of the store, left the shade down on its glass, and locked it again from the inside.

In the meantime, through the area Pilar had traversed half an hour earlier, workers were now pouring north, flooding the streets between tall, graceful gray palaces and huge movie houses with splendidly carved facades and posters behind glass announcing *Double Indemnity,* starring Fred MacMurray and Barbara Stanwyck and *Carta de un Enamorada,* with Bette Davis. The men from the Pampas were stupefied by the magnificence of what they saw.

The *descamisados* oohed and ahed over the goods in the sophisticated shop windows and admired the pretty, ornate streetlamps. As they moved, their ranks were swelled by other working stiffs seduced by the festive air of the marchers. Clerks from perfumeries and marble banking houses and the lowest-level functionaries in many of the businesses they passed joined in and went along with the happy men who had broken free for a day from the drudgery of their factories. God knows what they ate or drank. They did not care. Whatever else happened in the future, today they were free, today they were full of hope and wonder. By tens and twenties and then by fifties and hundreds, they converged on the Plaza de Mayo. As they neared the center, the lucky ones passed brother unionists from the printing industry, who handed them placards to carry.

Tulio Puglisi watched in amazement as thousands massed in the square. His eyes welled with tears. They were beautiful in their solidarity, so hopeful, so sure they were fighting on the side of right. But they could see only one path to their goal: Perón, a man who would use them. Exactly like the masses who hailed Hitler or Mussolini as their savior, they were drunk on hope brought to them by a scoundrel. The poor, naïve little shits were going to put a fascist in charge of Argentina. Tulio loved them, but they were totally wrong, and now no one could stop them.

While Puglisi feared destruction from the right, Lieutenant Ramón Ybarra was obsessed about a debacle coming from the other end of the spectrum: organized labor—in his mind, communists. He left his office and marched down the broad marble stairs and met his brother Ernesto at the main entrance to the Casa Rosada. He took him to the empty reception room near the rear door.

As usual, Ernesto sidled up to the subject with a lot of small talk about their mother and their sister. When Ramón couldn't stand it any longer, he forced his brother to the point. "This is no day for family small talk," Ramón said, with no attempt to disguise his impatience. "We have a tiger by the tail, and if we don't kill it, it will eat us all."

Ernesto winced as if he had been slapped. "Keep your voice down," he said. He looked over his shoulder and lowered his own tone to an annoying whisper. "I am here to save you from yourself. I tried to tell you the other night," he said, "about the GOU."

"I was a bit drunk to be truthful. *Grupo Obra de* something or other. Some kind of lodge of army officers. But how can you be thinking about some silly secret society from years ago while the pond scum of Argentina gather to bring down this city."

Ernesto looked around at the empty room again. "Please keep your voice down and listen to me. *Grupo de Oficiales Unidos.* I will explain again. It goes back at least to 1942, some say to the Mendoza garrison before then. Perón and Fárrell organized it with lovely words, saying it also stood for Government, Order, Unity, and the like." His tone was barely audible. "We were fighting communism, we thought, and defending Argentina's neutrality and independence. So we organized ourselves the way the communists organized themselves—to fight fire with fire, as they said—in small cells where the members knew only one another. Only military, no civilians."

Ramón thought he would explode. "Get to the point, Ernesto."

"Hear me out, Ramón. I've heard as many as two-thirds of the officers took an oath to support the GOU. Everyone's ticket to perfect mutual loyalty was to hand in a signed, undated letter of resignation. After that, GOU officers were maneuvered into the most powerful positions. There was a center of command—some vague cabal that none of us knew, except that Perón and Fárrell were at the center of it. The men just called it the Colonels' Clique."

"What has this got to do with today? The country is facing a worse threat than communism now, if you ask me."

"Please, Ramón, you have to be careful. We were all sworn to secrecy. That's why Avalos wouldn't talk to you himself."

"You are one of them?"

"I had just made captain. I felt honored that they asked me."

Ramón wanted to scream, but he held his tongue. His brother was an ass.

Ernesto went on, obviously exasperated now, but still he spoke barely above a whisper, which made Ramón pay close attention. "Once Fárrell became president, they dissolved the GOU, but no one ever got his resignation letter back. Everyone believes Perón still has them. He's got just about every senior officer in the army by the balls, little brother. No one is going to move against him, because everyone who has any power to command is hogtied by those letters."

Ramón backed against the wall, stupefied. Had Ernesto really told him all this the other night? Had he been that drunk that he had not heard it? Did Avalos know he had been stirring up his fellow officers at the garrison? He must. Someone had reported him. His intestines quaked. He sank down on one of the ornate settees covered with blue silk.

Ernesto sat beside him and blew out his breath. "The general has been trying to save you by getting me to tell you what he cannot say himself for obvious reasons."

"But—but—" Ramón sputtered. "If everyone is afraid of Perón, how come he let himself be arrested?"

Ernesto leaned even closer. "It is just the army that this applies to, Ramón. Not the other services. Not the civilians."

Ybarra's throat constricted. He could barely get his words out. "Ernesto, if today's revolt of the revolting works, Perón will reclaim power. Are you telling me the army is going to let that happen?"

Ernesto sat back and spoke almost normally. "There isn't going to be any opposition from the generals, Ramón." He put his hand on Ramón's forearm. "And there is going to be no putsch from Campo de Mayo. Fárrell and Avalos are going to let this drama play out, whatever it brings. And if you don't stop plotting to bring troops in the center and trying to get others to do the same, you are going to find yourself in one of those prison camps down in the Pampas or worse yet, falling from a plane into the ocean."

The image of falling stayed in Ybarra's mind throughout the next hour while he attempted to wrap his mind around the idea that the army, which he had expected would be the center of his life, was toothless. Not only toothless but in thrall to its most unworthy member: Perón. Perón.

It took Pilar that same hour to conclude that something was awfully wrong. The señora had not arrived at the store. Pilar had been telephoning her apartment every ten minutes or so but never received an answer. Lonely by herself with no real work to do, she tried calling Leary at his desk at police headquarters. He did not answer, but another man picked up the phone and took a message. "My name is Pilar Borelli," she said. "Please tell him that I am at the shop on Florida." She went back to filling bobbins and sorting patterns.

Evita Duarte had not even such mundane tasks to occupy her time while she waited for news of the dramatic events she knew must be taking place in the tense city center. She called her sister Erminda and Adele Nicolini to come and keep her company, but almost as soon as they arrived, they started to argue with each other about what Evita should be doing. Her sister favored an escape, getting Perón out of jail and then leaving for a life of peace and quiet somewhere far away from all the turmoil of Argentine politics. Adele said it was too late for that now; didn't Erminda understand that, with what was happening at that moment in the Plaza de Mayo, Perón would belong not to Evita alone but to the nation?

Evita paced the room and finally, unable to stand their effrontery for another moment, screamed at them, "You are arguing about my life. It is *my* life. Not yours to decide. *My* decision." She stalked into her bedroom and threw herself onto the bed. She knew exactly what should happen, but right now there was not a thing she could do but wait. She was not made to sit idly by at such a crucial moment.

Ybarra's mood perfectly matched that of the lady he abhorred, and he was equally frustrated by his inability to act. He had no friend or sister nearby at whom he could scream. Duty forced him to march with his general and a phalanx of guardsmen from Avalos's office to the president's sumptuous yellow room overlooking the stately plaza. Outside the french doors, down below the balcony, many thousands had already gathered beneath the palm trees and around the lovely monuments. As the shadows began to lengthen, the president's adjutant told them the police were estimating the crowd outside already at more than a hundred and fifty thousand. All those little animals out there, waving their placards and calling for that disgraceful bastard: "Perón. Perón."

Ybarra was helpless, and he knew it. Pilar, on the other hand, did not understand her own vulnerability when she heard a knock at the front door of the shop. She couldn't imagine it was a customer. Certainly Señora Claudia would let herself in with her key. It could only be Leary, and she ran to see. Before she unlocked the door, she moved the window shade that covered its glass, giggling, ready to make a funny face at him. She screamed. It was that man. In that same suit. The murderer, holding a knife! She ran to the telephone in the workroom as glass shattered behind her. He was on her back as she picked up the heavy black receiver. She swung it over her shoulder and smacked him in the head, but the blow glanced off his thick, brilliantined hair. He held the knife to her throat. She dropped the phone.

"You are a whore, just like that other one," he said in her ear.

In her terror, a picture fell into her head of the ladies from the church where she had gone as a child with her mother. They had called her mother a whore and said she would be one, too. That whores deserved to die.

"I saw you," he said, "kissing that man in his fancy car in front of this shop yesterday. Once I saw you I realized that you work here. You don't even feel your own shame, picking up fancy men in fancy cars."

"Please. You can't kill me for that? Please."

"I must," he said, fingering the handle of the knife, which he pointed at her throat. "You saw me the night I killed that other little whore. That one who had the gall to dress herself to look like a woman who is a saint. If people saw that little *puta* and thought she was Evita, they would think Evita was doing the disgusting things she did. People say that Evita is a whore. Evita blushes when she gets excited about something. How could she be a whore? Whores don't blush." He threw Pilar to the floor and stood over her with the knife pointed at her chest.

Terror shook her. "No, don't. Please."

He assessed her as if looking for the right place to stick his blade. Some vaguely engaged part of her brain silently argued with him. Luz had never done anything that Evita wasn't also doing. She bit her lip and cowered.

He spit at her, and his spittle landed on her cheek. Her stomach turned.

"Evita should be worshipped," he said. "And she will be one day. She was kind to that little tramp. Gave her dresses that were much too good for her. And the little *puta* used them imitate Evita, to make people think Evita was doing the disgusting things a whore would do."

"Luz loved Evita."

"Not the way I do," he said. "And you, you little slut. You made me betray her this morning when she really needed me. I saw you at the front door that night after the rally. I knew the other girl worked here. I saw her in that dress the day Evita gave it to her. But I didn't know who you were. I left Señora Evita alone because I had to find you." His eyes flashed, so angry that Pilar thought he would sink the knife into her at any second. "You knew it was me who killed that little slut. Now you have to die."

"Please," Pilar said. "I promise I will never say anything. I don't even know your name. I can't tell anyone. I swear. I will die before I will tell anyone."

He laughed. "I should just trust a whore like you? Not on your life." That made him laugh the more. "No. You will die before you have a chance to tell any—" A voice at the front door stopped his words.

"Get up," he said under his breath.

She leaped to her feet. She heard Señora Claudia's voice calling her name again from the front of the shop.

The murderer grabbed her arm and twisted it behind her back. He kept the knife at her throat. "Walk," he said and pushed her toward the door that led to the alley. Turning her to face them both toward the approaching voice, he reached behind him, unbolted the door, and dragged her through it. As he did, Señora Claudia came through the heavy velvet curtain that separated the workroom from the showroom. She screamed when she saw them.

"Follow me, and she's a dead girl," the murderer called to Claudia as he pushed Pilar into the alley, slammed the door behind them, and forced her to run to the end toward the side street.

As soon as they were out the door Claudia made to follow them, but at that moment a shout came from the front of the shop, and Roberto Leary ran into the room. "What's going on? I saw broken glass at the front door."

Claudia went to the back door. "Come quick," she said to Leary. "Eva Duarte and Juan Perón's chauffeur has taken Pilar. He has a knife."

With Roberto Leary at her heels, Claudia ran into the alley and followed the disappearing forms she saw silhouetted against the light where the narrow passage met the street.

While two desperate people flew down an alley and out into the *avenida* where throngs of men rushed toward the Plaza de Mayo, Ramón Ybarra sat imprisoned and impassive on a brown leather chair in the president's elegant office a few blocks away. He understood at last that his superior officers were empty uniforms, interested more in saving their positions of power than they were in securing the future of the country they had sworn to defend. A profound chill had settled on his insides. He no longer felt hot anger; his blood did not boil with the urge to take matters into his own hands, to foment a mutiny. Disillusion and fear for his own life froze his soul so deeply that not even Avalos's inane pronouncements moved him to speak out, much less act. A firing squad could await him. He could do nothing but watch, and hate, and follow orders.

As the sun began to set, Avalos repeated the pronouncement he had been making since Ybarra had returned, chastened, from his tête-à-tête with his brother. "The whole thing will melt away as soon as they see no one is paying enough attention to oppose them."

When a phone call came in saying that there were now at least three hundred thousand in the plaza and the surrounding streets, Avalos asked only if violence was being committed. When he hung up, he reported to the president, "Colonel Novara says the crowd is huge, but not at all violent. Joyous, really. The Buenos Aires police are refusing to attack the workers. Many of them seem to be siding with the demonstrators."

The president said nothing, but when Avalos spoke again, he seemed to be answering a question the president had forgotten to ask. He glanced into Ybarra's eyes and said, "I admit that the mob is much more powerful than we thought it would be, but we cannot send in the troops. I will not send my army into a bloody clash with the workers and the police. The army is already despised. We risk its entire future if we further alienate the populace."

Ybarra, of course, did not speak, but he did take special notice that Avalos had called them his army. But they really belonged to the man who held the undated letters of resignation: "Perón. Perón."

"You are right. It would be folly to turn this into a blood-bath." Fárrell spoke the words in the tone he would use to give a direct order. Ybarra resisted the urge to stand at attention and salute, which could only be interpreted as satiric.

"Evening has fallen," Avalos said. "I think it is time to send for Perón." He avoided his aide-de-camp's eyes. He picked up the phone and dispatched his own bulletproof car to the military hospital in the Belgrano district, just a few miles north of the Casa Rosada. The car had to plow through a crush of people, now so large it overflowed even the enormous Plaza de Mayo and jammed the nearby streets. It took much longer than the twenty minutes it should have to get there.

Amid that mob, with the murderer's arm around her and his knife, concealed by the sleeve of his jacket, pointed at her ribs, Pilar hurried obediently along Calle Sarmiento, and across Avenida San Martín. She tried to look behind her to see if Señora Claudia had followed them, but the horde of young men moving in the same direction made it impossible for her to see.

Her quaking heart crumbled. No one would ever find her in this multitude. A picture came out of nowhere, of children in trouble dropping a trail of bread crumbs so they would not get lost. She began to weep. "Shut up," the murderer said under his breath, as if she had spoken. "If you make a wrong move, my knife will be in your heart before you can let out a sound."

She began to shake, but two breaths later, when a group of young men hurried past them and they all turned down Reconquista toward the plaza, she realized that he could not do what he had threatened. If he stabbed her here, all these people would see him. He wanted to kill her so that she could not give testimony against him. What good would that do if scores of people saw him draw her blood? He could not hurt her and go free. He was stupid. She started to laugh hysterically and then, seeing the men around her start to pay attention to her, forced herself to laugh louder, so that they would stay focused on her. As they approached the plaza, she started to chant with the masses of men milling around them: "Perón. Perón."

All she had to do was wait out the murderer. Stay in the crowd. Find a way to keep attracting attention. That could not be so hard. There was not another girl in sight. Her heart so near his knife tried to tell her she was wrong. She was an inch from death. She clung to her hope. He wouldn't do it here. He was stupid for having taken her here. She tried to force herself to believe it.

Following behind, with no idea if he was going in the right direction, Roberto Leary wondered at how different his inner feelings were from his outward actions. His nerves were screaming in terror, but he moved like a machine, pushing through the crowd, following the dressmaker, desperate to find the man before he hurt Pilar— His mind stopped there. She was not going to die. She was not. It could not be. Having just found her, he could not lose her so soon.

Dusk was settling on the streets. In the half-light, as they moved toward the plaza and the chanting men, torches started to appear. The din of the crowd was joined by drumming on metal trash cans and clapping and shouting.

"There," Claudia Robles shouted. "That's her fuchsia scarf."

Leary saw no such thing, but he followed her as she plunged forward.

Claudia reached up and pulled the hat pin out of her hat. As they moved forward, the crowd became so thick that they could hardly move, but some people, seeing the hat pin in her hand, moved out of the way. If they hadn't, she was prepared to stab their stubborn backsides. Her eyes scanned the crowd. She could not see Pilar anymore. All she could do was swim as fast as she could through this sea of men, toward the spot where she had last seen the girl she refused to lose. She could not lose another one.

From Ybarra's perspective in President Fárrell's office, that sea looked more like an ocean. Avalos had turned off the bronze chandeliers. The only light came from sconces in the hallway. They were keeping the lights out to prevent the room from becoming the target of a Molotov cocktail. The lieutenant stood at the window of the dim room, staring out at thousands of dark heads, illuminated here and there by torchlight.

"There is nothing out there that looks dangerous at this moment," the president said over his shoulder to his minister of war.

"We cannot guarantee what will happen when darkness falls," Avalos said.

Ybarra was sure the animals would tear down the building if the day ended and they had not gotten their way. His superiors were about to be dealt the deathblow their own inaction had arranged. And once this was over, God only knew what they would do to him. He would very likely be arrested as a traitor. But, in fact, he was the only real patriot in this building at the moment.

"Where is our colonel?" Avalos asked, looking at his watch. None of them needed to define which colonel he meant.

"The bastard must be on his way from the hospital by now," Ybarra said.

Avalos's head snapped around, and he gave his aide what must have been a sharp look, if there had been enough light to see it. The ever-courtly Fárrell merely said, "Yes. I imagine you are right, Ramón."

A blaze went up outside the windows, near the fountain in the center of the mob. "Bonfire," Avalos said. "I wonder what they are finding for fuel."

Ybarra hoped it was the placards with the hated name. Even better if they burned one another. The spray from the fountain reflected the flames so it looked as if the water itself were burning.

"We have to stop this before they set fire to us," Fárrell

said. "Go down, Ramón, and hurry Perón up here as soon as he arrives."

Ybarra saluted, did an about-face, and marched smartly away from the weak fools who had signed away their power to Perón. They were treating Ybarra as if he had done nothing. He had conspired against them, and they did not even have the balls to accuse him. Yet. No matter how much he wanted them to be merciful to him, he could not get over their having done nothing against the real traitor to Argentina. "Perón. Perón."

Down in the mob, Pilar had no option but to obey when the murderer ordered her, "Sit down." She sank down in the middle of the crowd, near a bonfire. Though her heart palpitated, her brain was totally clear. He could not stab her here. He was confused about what to do. How could he kill her in full view of thousands, many of whom were taking an interest in the smiling, chanting girl being held close by a glum little man in a flashy suit, wearing a jacket and tie, as no one else around was.

To Pilar's complete disgust, her assailant sat behind her and wrapped his legs around her body. The men around them looked at her strangely. She took up their chant to get them on her side. If she could figure out a way to distract the murderer long enough to put some space between her ribs and his knife, they might help her subdue him. "Perón. Perón."

Not very far away, the darkness had stopped Hernán Mantell and his photographer colleague from taking any more photos of laborers climbing monuments and straddling the tops of lampposts. The photographer gave up and went back to his darkroom. Hernán made for the edge of the crowd to look for a pay phone so he could dictate copy to a stenographer in the typing pool in time for the early edition.

Less than fifty yards on the other side of Pilar, Claudia Robles plunged ahead with Leary right behind her. He was wishing that the Buenos Aires policemen carried guns. Not that he could fire in this crowd, but a pistol in his hand might get these dolts to move out of the way. Señora Robles's hat pin was a joke.

"Can you see her?" he shouted in her ear. She did not respond because she could not without stopping and turning around to make herself heard over the beating of drums and the chanting of the crowd: "Perón. Perón."

Evita, in her silent apartment, sang the chant in her heart and waited for news. The radio was useless, telling the same story over and over again, just enough to be tantalizingly hopeful, but not enough to answer as to the state of her colonel. "Perón. Perón."

She had long since sent her sister and Adele away. She paced, flopped into a chair for a few minutes, chewing her cuticles, then jumped up and paced some more. When the telephone rang, her nerves, already jangled from continually drinking coffee, flared and flamed. Miguel Angel Mazza's voice greeted her hungry ears.

"Señora," he said. "They have come to take Colonel Perón to the Casa Rosada. He is prepared to quell the uprising."

She gasped. "Will he be set free? Will he?"

"Oh, yes, I think so," Mazza said. "He is likely to come out of this reclaiming his place as the most powerful man in Argentina."

"Oh, thank Christ," she said. "Thank you so much. Thank you. Thank you."

She hung up and stood in the middle of the room hugging herself, feeling like a part of destiny, of his destiny. Of her country's destiny.

The top of her head tingled. She pictured the men she had spoken to quietly in the barrios two days ago. And those she had implored yesterday in the Plaza San Martín. *Bring ten more. Tell them each to bring ten more.* In her mind's eye, she saw them facing the pink palace among the statuary in the elegant Plaza de Mayo with its pyramid-shaped monument at the center, surrounded by banks, the old Cabildo, and the facade of the cathedral—like an ancient Greek temple. Ten of each of the faces she remembered, a hundred of each of them, chanting, "Perón. Perón."

The realization of her power seeped slowly into her brain, her lungs, her soul. Not everyone knew it yet. But she did. She had become a different person. This was it. This was the "it" she had longed for all her life, and now it was hers. She would never live in that old, poor, nasty world again. She was a new Evita.

When Perón, dressed in civilian clothes, arrived at the Casa Rosada, the negotiations between him and his former allies Fárrell and Avalos were carried out without rancor or even any hint of underlying tension. Officers and gentlemen behaved with the habits of a lifetime. Perón, now in perfect control of the situation, refrained from lording his triumph over vanquished men. There would be time for that later.

While polite bargaining took place in the palace, out in the plaza Pilar searched for a way to distract her assailant, who gripped her with his disgusting arms and legs. She could not bear being touched by this snake anymore. All the people close around her were also sitting on the ground. Just then, about ten yards to her left, in a group of people standing in a pool of light created by a streetlamp on the other side of the fountain, she saw a woman's hat—one she recognized as Señora Claudia's. If she could stand up and shout before the knife found her heart, the bonfire would give enough light to make her recognizable. She was sure the creep must feel the pounding of her pulse. The men nearest her were focused on the facade of the Casa Rosada, as if at any moment the man they called for would appear on the balcony. She tried staring at one of the demonstrators next to her, larger and stronger-looking than the rest, hoping to get him to look at her, but he would not.

Suddenly a light came on in a room on the second floor of the building they all faced—the room where the balcony was. As one person, the hundreds of thousands in the plaza, including the man who held the knife to Pilar's ribs, took in a breath. For a couple of seconds, the chanting stopped and everyone froze. Pilar jumped to her feet and shouted, "Help! Help me!"

Within an instant, he was up and grabbing at her, his knife flashing in the light of the bonfire. The men around her jumped up and stood there, frozen, while the murderer wrapped an arm around her and held his knife to her throat. "I will kill her if you come near us," he said. Suddenly, in the densely packed crowd a circle of space opened around them. Beyond that ring of shocked bystanders, in the ocean of humanity that surrounded them, the chant had resumed and reached delirium: "Perón. Perón."

None of the men who stared at her lifted a hand. Pilar knew she was dead. She could do nothing, except let him drag her through the crowd. If he wouldn't have killed her in front of them before, he would now. She thought of Leary. He had said he would protect her. But this was not his fault. He had told her to stay in his apartment. No one could help her now.

The already-packed crowd was trying to press closer to the balcony of the Casa Rosada. Inside the palace, under the now-lighted ornate chandeliers, the men who held the future of Argentina in their hands were coming to agreement. Perón would speak to the workers and persuade them to leave the center peacefully. The entire cabinet, what there was of it, would resign, including Avalos, and leave the next government to the voters in an election in February, an election they all knew Perón would win.

While the powerful men inside put the finishing touches on their pact, out in the gathering dark, bright pools of light from the torches and the bonfire had made searching the huge crowd for Pilar and her assailant increasingly difficult.

Leary's eyes had frantically scanned for her fuchsia scarf. He cursed himself for not staying with her. There were hundreds of thousands of people here. He despaired of finding her, and then there— His heart leaped. There, over a hundred heads of suddenly silent men sitting on the ground, silhouetted against the bonfire, she stood and shouted. Claudia saw her, too. They moved toward her, treading on some of the sitting men and shouting, "Stop him. Stop him." But by now the balcony doors had opened and the chanting had begun again. The workers were close to ecstasy. They felt it in their souls. Their demand was being heard. They were accomplishing something workers never had before all by themselves. They were forcing the government to listen. They had broken history and were remaking it. Many had taken off their shirts and were waving them over their heads at the man who stepped out onto the balcony. The *descamisados* were bellowing, "Perón. Perón."

Certain she had nothing to lose, Pilar let her body go limp. If her assailant was going to kill her, she was not going to make it easy. Let him do it here, in front of all these people. Maybe one of them would have a knife and kill the bastard in his turn.

All at once, Leary was blocking their way.

He took his hat off and crushed it around his left hand and went for the murderer. She felt the knife thrust and jammed her elbow between the blade and her ribs. The cut on her upper arm stung like fire. The murderer slashed the knife at Leary, who parried with the hand in the hat and punched the murderer in the face. A bystander handed Leary a knife. And suddenly that union man, Tulio Puglisi, was in the fight. And Señora Claudia was suddenly on top of the three men, stabbing with her hat pin and screaming.

Leary locked the murderer's head with his left elbow around the man's neck. The hat pin was dangling from his cheek. "She's bleeding," Señora Claudia shouted as soon as Pilar was free. She took the scarf from around Pilar's neck and bound the wound.

At that moment on the balcony, Perón raised his arms over his head. The crowd went delirious, men jumping up and down, shouting themselves hoarse: "Perón! Perón!"

Leary handcuffed the murderer. "Jorge. Jorge Webber," Señora Claudia said his name. She put her arm around Pilar.

"Help me get him out of here, Tulio," Leary said to the union man.

As they made their way to the edge of the sea of workers, up on the balcony the man of the moment embraced President Fárrell and raised his hands again to quiet the crowd. Their little group was too far away to hear what he was saying.

"Why did he kill her?" Señora Claudia asked.

Pilar looked at the miserable weasel and wanted to stomp him into mush on the spot. "He said Luz was a whore. That people say Evita is a whore, but she is a saint. That Luz imitating Evita would feed people's hatred of her, when they should revere her as a saint."

"God help us," Claudia said.

Tulio looked up at the man on the balcony who was flashing his famous smile at the crowd below. President Fárrell was waving and grinning. Perón basked in the kind of adulation he had not seen since his days in Mussolini's Rome and Hitler's Berlin. The workers thought they had won, but all of Argentina had lost. "Yes," Tulio said, "God help us."

As they reached the edge of the plaza, the crowd behind them began to sing the Argentine national anthem.

Leary commandeered a squad car to take Pilar to the hospital. As he threw Webber into another car to be taken to police headquarters, the workers started to chant again, "Perón. Perón."

"Someday," Webber shouted, "they will be chanting 'Evita. Evita.'" He continued to chant, "Evita! Evita!"

"God help us," Tulio said again.

MONDAY, OCTOBER 22

Among the resignations that President Edelmiro Fárrell had to deal with in the aftermath of the events of October 17 was the departure from the army of Lieutenant Ramón Ybarra. Having been saved from a death sentence by the good offices of General Avalos, without further inducement he chose to pursue another career. Unlike many of his fellow officers, Ybarra wrote his resignation, signed, dated, and handed it in all on the very same day. By the following Friday, he was packing to move to Mendoza, in the foothills of the Andes far from the capital, where his mother's brother was a prominent member of the Basque Diaspora community and the proprietor of a wine-making operation that had more than tripled in size during the war in Europe, when importing wine had been impossible. Other anti-Perón officers, fearing that the triumphant colonel still held their original letters of resignation, wrote new ones and left the army. Many removed to Montevideo, Uruguay, to bide their time until they might return to their native land. They got their wish in less than a decade. Others stayed and prepared to knuckle under to their former colleague's dominance.

In the meantime, on October 22, in a civil ceremony in Junín, the town where Evita grew up, Perón married his actress. The colonel felt free to take this wife now that he was so powerful that no one's disapproval could hurt him. He was free at last to unleash the full force of her charisma on his behalf.

For the ceremony, he wore his full dress uniform. She dressed in the lovely polka-dotted ensemble that Claudia Robles had designed for Perón's fiftieth-birthday celebration, but she also sported the dreaded white hat with the cabbage roses.

Perón would go on to be the president and dictator of Argentina and she his first lady. The poor little girl had grown up to be such a somebody that a couple of years later, on her first trip to Europe, General Franco of Spain—who shared much of her husband's political philosophy—sent his private DC-4 to fly her to Madrid, escorted by a squadron of forty planes from the Spanish air force. In Paris, dressed by Dior, she stood on the carpeted pedestal and looked at her blond self in the triple mirror. The woman in the gorgeous gown was her! No longer the little worm that people had crossed the street to avoid when she was a bastard girl out on the Pampas in Los Toldos. She was a butterfly at last. Her face flushed with joy, and her heart swelled to become the heart of the woman she had always wanted to be.

But Evita's basking in the light of fame lasted only seven years. She died at the age of thirty-three, by which point she was the most famous woman in the world and already a legend.

In the immediate aftermath of the events of October 17, public and private, Luz's grandmother, in deep mourning over the death of her son, failed to claim her granddaughter's body. When Leary found out that the girl's corpse still lay refrigerated in the morgue, he enlisted Ireno Estrada to help him steal it. He and Claudia Robles, Hernán, and Señor Gregorio gave Luz a hastily arranged funeral on Saturday, October 20. In the cemetery of La Recoleta, at the mausoleum where Claudia's grandmother was buried. Gregorio, his blue eyes bright with emotion, gave an impassioned eulogy about how parents and grandparents should protect their offspring. His words were more stirring than any priest's could have been.

In the late afternoon on the day of Evita's wedding, Roberto Leary drove his red Pontiac into the hospital parking lot, swearing to himself that if the doctors did not let Pilar go home today, he would kidnap her. They had said she would be there for three days when she went in. It had turned into five. The cut in her arm was deep and had required many stitches. She had needed a transfusion. He and Claudia Robles, and even Tulio Puglisi, had offered to donate their blood, and the hospital had taken some from all of them, because with all the gunfights in the city over the past weeks, the supply was very low.

By Friday afternoon, Pilar had seemed infinitely better and complained bitterly about being kept in her bed. But the doctors insisted that they needed to be sure the wound would not suppurate. With the war barely over in the Pacific, there were no supplies of the miracle drug penicillin to cure infections. Suppose she lost her arm, Leary berated himself. He should never have left her. No matter what was going on in the city, he should have stayed only with her. He knew it was silly of him to think so. But everything about her intoxicated him. Besides, what had he done that day anyway? Lower a bridge so a bunch of harmless, little, skinny working stiffs wouldn't drown in the Riachuelo? None of the cops had done anything much but watch. The docs in the hospital had said the seventeenth had been an incredibly quiet day for injuries, especially considering the violence of the past months. They were shocked to find that the only person who had gotten seriously hurt among the estimated three hundred and fifty thousand demonstrators was a girl.

Leary approached her room and saw Hernán Mantell standing outside the closed door. "Claudia is in there helping her get dressed," he said.

They stood in silence for a moment. "I'm taking her home with me," Leary said. "I feel like I never want to let her out of my sight again."

Mantell nodded. "I can believe it."

The door opened, and Pilar stood just inside the hospital room, smiling. She had heard Leary's voice when he arrived, heard him say that he was taking her home with him. Now, she saw admiration in his eyes. Señora Claudia had designed and made with her own hands a beautiful dress for Pilar to wear, of silk in the palest yellow, with a slim skirt and a full draped top, to accommodate her arm in a sling beneath. It was, by far, the most beautiful thing she had ever owned. The señora had done her makeup, brushed her hair. She felt beautiful, like a bride in her traveling outfit, setting off for Paris. She had sewn clothes like these for girls who got to do such things. But she was happy to go with Leary to his flat in San Telmo and stay there with him as long as he would have her.

He stepped to her and kissed her on both cheeks. "Are you okay?"

"No sign of infection. It's a good thing. What good would a one-armed seamstress be?" She meant it as a joke, but none of them laughed, and the tears that she had kept at bay for five days suddenly burst out of her eyes.

"Oh no!" Claudia said. She grabbed a towel from a rack next to the sink to catch the drops. "Please don't let them fall on the silk." Then she was weeping, too. For poor little Luz, to whom she had said those identical words in an incident that led directly to the girl's death.

"What do we do with them, Mantell?" Leary asked. "Now, they are crying. Now that everything is alright."

Hernán put his arm around Claudia's shoulders. He knew

why she wept, and why often it was only when relief came that she let herself go.

"I have a nice bottle of Torrantes chilling in my refrigerator," Leary said. "Won't you come and share it with us?"

"Oh, please do," Pilar said. She wanted Señora Claudia to see how nice his place was.

When they were settled in his parlor with their wine and a platter of antipasti from the Sicilian grocers, they talked about the meaning of all they had seen in the last fateful days.

"I used to think," Leary confessed, "that Perón might be a good thing for Argentina. That was what most of the guys on the force thought. But for all I've heard in the past week, whatever good he does will come at too high a price."

"The men I work with at the paper are talking about leaving the country. There is no way we will be able to report the truth. Anyway, our paper won't survive the crackdown."

Pilar gasped. "Oh, Señora Claudia, you are not thinking of leaving Buenos Aires, are you?" She thought about her work, that her job would disappear.

Claudia smiled. "I think it's time for you to drop the 'señora' and address me in the familiar. And, no. I will stay. I cannot move my father, so I cannot go."

Hernán took her hand. "And so will I," he said. "I will find a way to earn a living with my pen. Someday, I hope, eyewitness accounts of what we have just seen will be needed."

Leary put his arm gingerly around Pilar's shoulders and kissed her cheek. "Perón is pretty sure to win the next election. It will take until after that before the worst oppression takes hold. That's what Tulio Puglisi says. The voting isn't until February. In the meantime, I will do my job. After that, I won't want to be a cop."

"What about that nice union man, Tulio?" Pilar asked. "What's going to happen to him?"

"He has to get out of Argentina before the arrests and intimidation begin," Hernán said. "He told me he might go back to Sicily, where his parents came from. Or to a cousin in Pennsylvania."

He turned to Leary. "What about that son of bitch Webber? Do you think Perón will get his chauffeur off?" Hernán asked.

"I called Señora Duarte to tell her what had happened," Leary said. "She said she hopes he rots in jail, that he abandoned her when she needed him most."

Pilar laughed. "So much for Evita the Saint."

Claudia wondered if she would ever be asked to make another dress for the tiny actress. "She will probably go to the French designers now that she is going to be the president's wife," she said aloud, not really intending to.

They all laughed. But then a sad silence fell. "What will become of Buenos Aires now?" Claudia asked. "I am afraid for my city if it is under mob rule."

"Not the mob," Hernán said. "Perón. Perón." He imitated the chants of the workers in the plaza. "And he is worse than the mob. We are in for terrible times."

Claudia sighed deeply. "Oh, God, don't say that."

Hernán took her hand. "Dearest, there has been a city

here for four hundred years," he said. "It has survived dreadful times before. Rome survived Caligula. Buenos Aires will survive Perón."

"One day, perhaps," Leary said, not entirely in jest, "Pilar and I will move to Paris and open a school of the tango there."

Pilar's heart wobbled. She imagined how wonderful that would be.

"In the meantime," Leary said, "we'll stay here in the city we love, and we'll dance."

He went to the Victrola in the corner and wound it. He put a record on the turntable and put the needle in the groove. The velvety voice of Carlos Gardel filed the room, singing "Mi Buenos Aires Querido." The two couples stood in the small space between the back of the sofa and the door. They held one another in close embrace, not dancing, for there was not enough room, but feeling the music in their bodies.

HISTORICAL NOTE

This is a work of fiction. The background events are given more or less as they happened, but the historical characters are presented in a fictional way—to serve the story rather than the facts. The details of what they say and do should not be taken as historically accurate.

The tumultuous politics of Argentina at this dramatic moment seemed best portrayed by creating characters that embodied the various points of view. The character of Evita was the hardest to peg. Contemporaneous accounts and most biographers portray her either as a saint or a whore. She appears to this writer as neither and as both. She was a woman driven to overcome her sad and hopeless childhood; her biting ambition had its roots in humiliating poverty. But those bleak early years also made her a true believer when it came to championing the underdog. Though I do not approve of the repressive regime of the man she loved and supported with all her heart, though she was often a self-serving viper, Evita is, in some ways, irresistible. Imperfect virago, naïve and ill educated, still she was a genuine idealist who believed with all her heart that Perón was bringing social justice to the poor workers of Argentina. She worked tirelessly to help the downtrodden of her country, albeit with little regard to the niceties of charitable fund-raising or transparent accounting. That said, she did build hospitals and schools and trained record numbers of nurses. Where other, worthier champions of women's suffrage failed (notably Alicia Moreau de Justo), as first lady, Evita succeeded in getting women the vote. She and Perón saw to it that Perón got the credit. In fact, Evita may have invented the role of first lady—the activist wife of a head of state.

I believe Perón was a master manipulator who exploited Evita's ignorance, passionate nature, and craving for stardom, as he did Argentina's economic and social problems, to achieve and keep his powerful grip on his beleaguered nation. For her part, having attained power as President-General Perón's wife, she wielded it with a vengeance. Once they were a first couple, Evita became very much the center of attention. She protested constantly that she was only a conduit between the people and the man who was really responsible for their gains. But Perón immediately began to lose power after she died; his first regime lasted less than three more years. Was he the weaker of the two, goaded to greatness by her ambition, the beneficiary of her love and charisma?

Or was he the wizard behind the curtain who used her showy involvement to mask his real machinations and distract attention from the brutality of his stranglehold on Argentina?

It seems impossible that anyone will ever tease away the myth and reveal the real Evita. But this I know for sure: Evita's early experiences taught her to hate the ruling class. At least some of them lived up to her assessment, in spades. When at the age of thirty-three she lay dying a tortured death of a uterine malignancy, they scrawled "Long Live Cancer" on the walls in their fancy neighborhoods. How can one refuse a certain amount of sympathy to a dying young woman so abused?